The Yellow Farce

A New Sherlock Holmes Mystery

Note to Readers:

Your enjoyment of this new Sherlock Holmes mystery will be enhanced by re-reading the original story that inspired this one –

The Yellow Face

It has been appended and may be found in the back portion of this book. <u>But</u> if you have never read it or cannot remember it, then do not read it first, since it will be a spoiler.

Dear Reader:

You can have your name in print.

Would you like to be a character in a future New Sherlock Holmes Mystery? I will use your name for: a hero (other than Holmes or Watson), a heroine, a victim (Careful on this one. You might not survive), a police inspector, a secondary bad guy, a secondary good guy, a servant or other minor character.

If you do, then send me your name as you want it to appear and the type of character you would like to be to: CraigStephenCopland@gmail.com and I will let you know when you are going to appear.

AND

Do you want to receive notice of each New Sherlock Holmes Mystery when it is published? And hear about all free and discounted books?

Yes? Then please do any or all of the following:

Follow me on Bookbub here:

www.bookbub.com/profile/craig-stephen-copland?list=author_books

Follow "Craig Stephen Copland" and "New Sherlock Holmes Mysteries" on Facebook

Follow me on Amazon Author Central here:

amzn.to/2JOJVvt

Warm regards,

CSC

The Yellow Farce

A New Sherlock Holmes Mystery

Craig Stephen Copland

Published by:

Conservative Growth Inc.
3104 30th Avenue, Suite 427
Vernon, British Columbia, Canada
V1T 9M9

Cover design by Rita Toews.

ISBN 13:   978-1534608351

ISBN: 1534608354

Dedication

To those tens of thousands of people throughout the nation of Japan who are dedicated Sherlockians, especially to my friend, colleague and fellow pastiche writer, Hugh Ashton – *il miglio fabbro*.

Dear Reader:

You can have your name in print.

Would you like to be a character in a future New Sherlock Holmes Mystery? I will use your name for: a hero (other than Holmes or Watson), a heroine, a victim (Careful on this one. You might not survive), a police inspector, a secondary bad guy, a secondary good guy, a servant or other minor character.

If you do, then send me your name as you want it to appear and the type of character you would like to be to: CraigStephenCopland@gmail.com, and I will let you know when you are going to appear.

AND

Do you want to receive notice of each New Sherlock Holmes Mystery when it is published? And hear about all free and discounted books?

Yes? Then please do any or all of the following:

Follow me on Bookbub here:
www.bookbub.com/profile/craig-stephen-copland?list=author_books

Follow "Craig Stephen Copland" and "New Sherlock Holmes Mysteries" on Facebook

Follow me on Amazon Author Central here:
amzn.to/2JOJVvt

Warm regards,

CSC

Contents

Acknowledgments

Like all writers of Sherlock Holmes fan fiction, I owe a debt to Sir Arthur Conan Doyle. Or, if you are a true Sherlockian, to Dr. John Watson, who recorded the brilliant exploits of the world's most famous detective. This particular story is a tribute to the original story, *The Yellow Face*. It was thoughtfully pointed out to me that the use of the word 'Yellow' in a story about Japan could be misconstrued as a racial slur. That possibility was not intended, nor had it even occurred to me.

In all my stories, I drop in unacknowledged quotes and references as tributes to other writers and events. I hope you enjoy spotting them as much as I did inserting them. Of special note is the Russian math professor, whose story has been directly lifted from the brilliant satirist, Tom Lehrer. You can still buy it online.

A special thanks is given to my dear friend, Mary Engelkling, who, generously supplied all of the Russian language insertions and continues to encourage my writing. My fellow scribblers who are part of *Write Together in Iidabashi* enlightened me concerning the famous Japanese legend of the Bamboo Cutter, and I thank them. Many friends and acquaintances, both Japanese and ex-pat, have contributed to my elementary knowledge of Japanese language, culture, and history.

Several friends read draft versions of this story and made valuable edits and suggestions, mostly related to sections that needed to be cut. My thanks to all of them. And again, I acknowledge the dear friends and family who continue to encourage me in this pleasant if quixotic quest of writing a new mystery to correspond to every story in the original Canon.

Chapter One

Murder in the Orient, Expressed

Oh, to be in England
Now that April's there,

The above lines are utter nonsense, penned by one of our pampered, whinging poets as he cavorted in sunny Italy. The only way that April can ever be said to be pleasant in England is by comparison with the months of January, February, and March, which are consistently cold, damp, and beastly miserable and thus marginally worse than April. The only way that the month of April 1905, was pleasant for Sherlock Holmes and me was that we were *not* in England. We were on the other side of the earth attending to one of the most complex cases that had ever presented itself to the mind of the world's most famous detective—the dangerous quest for the prized yellow ribbon, the splendid yellow kimono, and the priceless golden arrow.

For over two months, from New Year's Day, 1905 on, the drizzle, sleet, fog, and wind had not let up. Having retired from my regular medical practice, I had no excuse to leave and go to my surgery each morning. My beloved wife, tragically, passed away the previous year, and I had, in retrospect, not wisely, moved back in to share rooms with my friend and closest companion, Sherlock

Holmes, the now famous—as a result of my stories about him—consulting detective. We had become two cranky bachelors, both beyond middle-aged, and it had become a chore not to find each other annoying.

Holmes was inevitably irascible whenever there were no interesting cases in his docket. Over the Christmas season, he had cleared the name of poor old Mrs. Rachel Abernetty, who Scotland Yard had accused of murdering her son-in-law. Holmes had proven that choking to death on Christmas pudding had a long and distinguished history in the annals of English tragedies and could not be blamed on the preparer of the dish, regardless of how greatly she despised the consumer.

For the past three weeks, however, there had been nothing, and, in addition to indulging in his longstanding habit of tobacco, he had gone so far as using his dangerous seven percent solution to relieve the monotony of existence. It was this turn of events that forced me to take strong measures for the protection of his health. The opportunity arose on a Sunday in early March, where that rarest of English events occurred, a glorious sunny morning.

I insisted that we bestir ourselves and take a walk through the Park and refused to consider any objection he could offer. I prevailed, and the two of us donned our ulsters and proceeded a short block north on Baker Street and entered Regent's Park. Unfortunately, we were not the only Londoners to have been struck with this idea. We escaped the families, children, and barking dogs and found a quiet bench close by the rugby pitch. He sat silently, lit his beloved pipe, and enjoyed a few minutes of solemn contemplation. The scowl had not departed from his face, and I sought in vain to find something to say that would cheer him up.

"You must admit, Holmes," I tentatively offered, "that the sight of young English families, with their happy dogs and children, enjoying themselves in the sunshine, restores some optimism for the future of the human race."

"I will admit no such thing, my good doctor. I concluded many years ago that a man who cannot stand either dogs or children cannot be all bad."

"Oh, come, Holmes. I am quite sure that somewhere in the corner of your hard heart, there is some love for both children and animals."

"Children must be tolerated since without them the future of the human race would be in jeopardy. As to animals, you are quite correct, Watson. I do love animals. They are delicious."

I laughed in spite of myself. "Holmes, you cannot be that cynical. You must acknowledge that animals have a special place in the lives of an English family."

"I do, indeed, so acknowledge. And that special place is beside the mashed potatoes and underneath the Yorkshire pudding."

I was about to upbraid him until I caught the faint trace of a smile at the corner of his lips, a sure sign that his spirits had begun to soften.

We walked back to 221B Baker Street but did so by avoiding the crowded pathways and marching across the open fields. The ground was soft but quite walkable. The grass had a soft hue of green to the emerging shoots, the chestnuts were preparing to burst out in five-fold leaves, and scattered hither and thither were joyful tiny crocuses. The effect was irresistible, and even Sherlock Holmes could not stop his disposition from turning to the light. We chatted on about some of the events of the day and the latest on our king-sized King, and so on. By the time we had reached our abode, he was positively cheerful.

That mood vanished when we arrived at our door. Parked on the street in front of it was a finely appointed carriage, bearing the insignia of the Government of Great Britain. Its presence could only mean one thing—that some high-ranking official of His Majesty's Government was waiting to meet with Sherlock Holmes. Before we grasped the handle of the door, it swung open in front of us, and standing in the doorway was our dear Mrs. Hudson, her face ashen, bordering on terrified.

"Mr. Holmes, she said in a trembling whisper, "it's your brother."

Holmes smiled warmly at her. "Is it now? And is he happy?"

"Why, no, Mr. Holmes. He is not happy at all. I offered him tea and even some of your best brandy. But he just glowered at me and grunted and bade me leave him alone."

"Why then, he must be in a good mood. If he were in a bad mood, he would be ripping pages out of my books or adulterating my chemical experiments. Take no heed of him, my dear lady. Come, Watson, nothing like a sunny day to go and poke the bear."

He bounded up the seventeen stairs with a bit of a spring in his step. I had learned over the years that the intense sibling rivalry between these two towering howbeit non-conformist intellects was something that each of them secretly enjoyed. There existed a mutual if grudging respect, much as is common between two prizefighters who have just knocked each other silly for sixteen rounds.

"Ah, my dear brother," beamed Holmes as he strode into the room. "How sweet of you to drop by. If you came to wish me a happy birthday, I fear you are two months late. Ah ha, it must be the approaching Easter season. And my warmest Christian blessings to you as well, Mycroft. I know just how deeply you are touched by the Resurrection of our Lord."

"Sherlock," the oversized presence in the room snapped, "Where have you been? I have been waiting for over half an hour. Perhaps you have time to waste, but I do not."

He did not rise from the sofa to greet his brother, which, given his now unhealthy girth, was not surprising. At one time, he bore facial features that were similar to his younger sibling's, but now the effects of too much rich food and a total absence of exercise had taken their toll. He was the same height as Sherlock Holmes, but at least three stone, maybe four beyond him in weight. Getting up out of comfortable sofas was not a comfortable task for Sir Mycroft Holmes.

"On my doctor's orders," continued Holmes with feigned cheerfulness, "I have been taking my exercise for exercise's sake in the Park. This good doctor is concerned about my health and my weight."

While the part about his health was certainly true, the only concern I had for his weight was the lack of it. He had not an ounce of fat on his trim body, not as a result of bodily exercise but of eating no more than was necessary to keep him alive. Our dear Mrs. Hudson had tried in vain over a quarter of a century to "put some meat on his bones," but it had been for naught.

"Sherlock, cut the nonsense," snapped Mycroft. "If anyone were to look at you, they would think that a famine had swept the country."

"Oh, how right you are, my dear brother. Of course, if they were to look at you, they would know the cause. But enough of our respective situations of health; do tell me to what it is then that I owe the honor of your visit."

"Stop playing the fool. You know perfectly well that I would only come here if there were a danger to the Empire with the potential for dire consequences. Otherwise, I have better things to do. Now sit down and listen."

I made as if to retire discreetly to my bedroom, although I was inwardly dying to hear what was about to be said.

"Watson," barked Mycroft Holmes. "Sit down. I am going to need to have complete reports on this assignment, and my brother is too conceited to admit that it is not sufficient to rely on one's memory when matters of state are at stake. Sit down, and take out your blessed notebook."

I did as ordered.

"There is," he continued, "as I assume the two of you have read, a war in the Far East."

I volunteered a response. "Between the Russians and the Japanese, you mean. But we are neutral, are we not? How does it concern His Majesty if Britain is not involved?"

Mycroft gave me a scornful look.

"Yes, we are officially neutral, in spite of our Alliance with the Japanese, and it does matter to us what is going on over there. The outcome is of enormous consequence."

"Well then, brother," said Holmes, "Kindly state your case. Furnish me with the facts. I am all attention."

Mycroft leaned back in the sofa and crossed his arms across his large, well-padded chest.

"It concerns our envoy in Tokyo. I assume that you know to whom I am referring."

I racked my memory and could not come up with anything, but I knew that Sherlock Holmes read every major newspaper every day and forgot nothing. His answer did not surprise me.

"Ah, yes. A bright young chap named Grant Munro. Cambridge about fifteen years back. Took some prizes and a first. That chap? To be blunt, Mycroft, I cannot imagine a fine young guy from Cambridge ever becoming a problem. All budding young Kimball O'Haras and loyal to the Empire, are they not?"

"Cut the sarcasm. Yes, that's him. He sat the Foreign Service exam and did brilliantly. His career to date has been stellar, and before he had turned thirty, he was made a full Envoy in East Africa. Did wonderful work overseeing the construction of the Mombasa-to-Uganda railway. Very fine work."

"I would have thought," countered Holmes, with a straight face, "that those workers who were eaten by lions at Tsavo might beg to differ with you."

"That was overblown by the press," said Mycroft. "We only lost a mere half dozen before the lions were hunted down. From the accounts in the papers, you would have thought that the entire company had been devoured. After that one unfortunate incident, the construction continued all the way to Lake Victoria. A brilliant piece of work. So much so that in 1900 he was awarded the post in Tokyo, which is quite the plum appointment for so young a diplomat."

"Very impressive," agreed Holmes. "So wherein is the problem?"

"His wife. He went and got married out on the field."

"Oh, dear. Well, now, that is a problem. I assume it was what your insufferable snobs over in Whitehall, who still believe in the superiority of the white race, would call *going native*. Did the young man acquire a bad case of *jungle fever*, as you call it?"

"No. He did not get married until after he arrived in Japan."

"Oh, well, that's not quite so serious. Only a case of *yellow fever*. I believe that is the Whitehall term for it..."

"Blast you, Sherlock," Mycroft interrupted. "He married an American missionary."

"Ah, well, that is a relief. Merely a common case of Yankee Panky. Invigorating for the constitution, although known to be fatal to the bank account. Tell us about his wife and her missionary position. How could any such Christian lady be a concern?"

"The first concern is that for several days every fortnight, she keeps disappearing without saying where she is going, and not revealing where she has been. Secondly, every month, substantial sums appear in her bank account from an unknown source."

"Oh, my. I really cannot think of more than half the married men on earth who would not be on their knees thanking whatever gods they believe in were their wives to do likewise and not be making endless demands for more money. How lucky can a man be? Pray tell, why is this a problem?"

"It is a problem," Mycroft said testily, "because she is a Russian."

"You just said that she was an American."

"She *is* an American. She was born and raised in New Jersey. But her family emigrated from Vladivostok in 1860. They joined the Baptist Church in Hoboken and the Freemasons and sent their children to the local public school, but they made sure that they could all speak Russian. And you know what that means."

"I confess that I do not. Pray, explain."

"Really, Sherlock, your naiveté with respect to international affairs disappoints me. It means that no matter what happens, you cannot get rid of the *Russia* within a Russian. Their loyalty to Mother Russia will always be there, regardless of what country they live in or how many generations removed."

"I confess that I did not know that. Please, continue."

"This woman, Ekaterina—or Effie for short—Federova, did well in school, decided that the Almighty had called her to the mission field, became a nurse, and at the tender age of nineteen off she went to save the Japanese heathen. She remained a spinster, admired and respected by all who knew her until she was thirty-eight, whereupon she met our star envoy, Munro, at a diplomatic function. They fell in love and were married within three months. No sooner had the honeymoon ended than she began her inexplicable disappearances, and they have continued unabated."

"My dear brother, I cannot believe that you departed from your *sanctum sanctorum* over in Whitehall and condescended to visit me just because some evangelizing American Baptist nurse has been acting strangely. Perhaps you could further enlighten me."

"If that were all there was to it, you know I would not be here. It so happens that in the past three months, our cultural attaché has disappeared. Vanished, without a trace. And just yesterday, we learned that the Deputy Head of Mission at the American Embassy was found floating in the river, having suffered a rather nasty scratch on his throat. That is why I am here. We believe that all of these events are connected and that somehow Envoy Munro's wife is involved."

Holmes's eyes involuntarily widened. His hands came together under his chin, and he pressed his fingertips together. "Mycroft, you have a network of agents all over the world, better known as *spies,* who should be able to look into these matters for you. Surely, you have contacts within the Tokyo Legation. Why are you here talking to me?"

"Of course, I have some of my people in Tokyo, but it is precisely because they are spies that I cannot afford to use them. They are trained as professional diplomats, which means that they are the finest group of young *liars* in the Empire. On such a sensitive matter, they will invariably tell me what they think I want to hear. I would have no way of knowing if their reports were true or not."

"Then use some of your old hands in Whitehall. Are they not veterans of the field and experienced in all manner of skullduggery and legerdemain?"

"Exactly, which makes them the finest group of *old* liars. And regardless of how endlessly annoying I find it to have a conversation with you, I know that you are incapable of looking me in the eye and lying. And that is why you are being sent off to Japan. You have two days to pack. And take your Boswell with you. I need to have complete written reports even if they are sensationalized and romanticized. You depart on Wednesday. And don't claim that you are occupied with some intricate case. Your docket is empty."

Holmes sat back and was quiet. I had reached the conclusion that I would soon be on my way to the Land of the Rising Sun, a prospect that, I must admit, I found rather pleasing.

"I presume," said Holmes, "that you have concocted some pretense for my visit. It really would not do to have me arrive as the official investigator of the Envoy's wife."

"Of course not. You are part of a cultural exchange. The Legation will be hosting a display of British *objets d'art*. We've tossed in a few Gainsboroughs, Turners, and Stubbs; a copy of the Magna Carta, the Domesday Book, the Rosetta Stone, a selection of the Crown Jewels and goodness knows what else. Oh yes, some of our recently departed Queen's dresses. The Japanese just adore the old girl. The British Empire is sponsoring a set of vigorous athletic races, and, for good measure, we are throwing you in as well."

"Permit me to remind you, my dear brother, that I am a professional consulting detective, not some exhibit you can stuff and mount and pin to the wall."

"In Nippon, Sherlock, that is exactly what you are. Thanks to Watson, the stories of your investigations have been translated and sold all over Japan. There is a Sherlock Holmes Society now with several thousand members who meet regularly ... oh, pardon me ... *irregularly* ... to discuss your adventures. For no reason that I can possibly understand, they are besotted with you. I fully expect that you will be mobbed with admirers in every one of your public lectures. You will have three weeks on board one of P & O's liners to prepare. Thomas Cook will deliver your ticket. A set of files will be delivered here on Tuesday that you will have to have mastered before your arrival in Tokyo. You will arrive in time to enjoy *Hanami,* provided that you are not mistaken for a fishing trawler by the Russian Fleet."

Without bidding us good-day, he lifted his bulky frame from the sofa and departed.

Chapter Two   West then East of Eden

Although several decades had passed since my service in the Northumberland Fusiliers, I had not forgotten the art of packing lightly and quickly and being ready to break camp on an hour's notice. Before the evening had passed, I was ready to go. So, for the next two days, I prowled the bookshops searching for anything that might render Japan a less completely unknown entity. In Hatchards on Piccadilly, I found a recent edition of Baedeker's blue guides, which announced that it would tell me all I needed to know about the island nation of the Far East.

I read it from cover to cover and diligently practiced bowing to the mirror while smiling and saying useful phrases such as *ohayo gozaimasu,* or *arigato gozaimasu,* or *konnichiwa,* I imagined myself courteously bowing to a distinguished shogun and respectfully pronouncing "Arigato Gozaimaaaas."

Holmes, on the other hand, buried himself in reports in the press and in dossiers sent over from Whitehall regarding the hostilities between Russia and Japan and the complicated relationship of Great Britain with each of them.

"Very well, now, Holmes," I teased him on the Tuesday evening. "Which of the two are our friends? Or is the correct answer *neither*?"

He put down the file he was reading and shook his head. "The only certain answer would be 'a plague on both your houses.' Japan is currently on good terms with us since we are buying their silk by the boatload and selling them a navy. We have been skirmishing with the Russian bear for five decades in the Great Game throughout the *Stans*, but we cooperated on the Boxer rebellion. Then back in October, we mobilized the Fleet and were almost at war with them after some imbecile admiral of theirs sunk our fishing trawlers on the Dogger Bank. Frankly, I can make neither head nor tail of it, and I rather suspect that even Mycroft must find it confusing."

"Ah yes," I agreed, "but then we denied their warships the use of our Suez. So even if we leave tomorrow, we shall beat their fleet to Japan."

"We shall, indeed," said Holmes. "And then goodness only knows what duplicity will await us."

On the Wednesday morning, Holmes and I rose early and found a cab to the Tilbury Wharf. Once there, we made our way to the S.S. Delhi, the newest liner in the gleaming P&O fleet, boarded, and were escorted to a select cabin in the first-class section. As I looked it over in profound delight, I could not help but remember my ocean voyage of many years ago on the troop-ship Orontes. My health was broken, and I was near death the entire way back from the Sub-Continent, having been wounded in the war and only barely kept alive by the valiant efforts of Murray, my orderly. The conditions I would be enjoying over the next few weeks could not have been further removed from those miserable days of my youth.

Shortly after we had settled in our cabin, a knock came to the door. Two Royal Marines confirmed that we were indeed Sherlock Holmes and Dr. John Watson and, having done so, presented us with a secured diplomatic case and the necessary set of keys. Over the next three weeks, I would read through the documents before nearly dying of boredom and retreating to the liner's library and bar.

Holmes, I knew, would read and re-read them until he had committed every word to his prodigious memory.

The weather improved greatly as we rounded Gibraltar and steamed non-stop to Port Said and the mouth of that great marvel of engineering, the Suez Canal. An Englishman could not help but smile at how the French had enslaved the Egyptians and together labored and died by the thousands in its construction, only to have the British Crown snap it up for a few pennies on the pound when the *Compagnie universelle du canal maritime de Suez* fell on hard times and went bankrupt. And now, on maps of the world, the Canal is a glorious red.

Telegrams and diplomatic pouches were waiting for Holmes at Port Said. The Russian Fleet, on route to the Far East, was bottled up in Madagascar while the French colonial dockhands worked, on French time, no doubt, to re-supply the ships with coal and provisions. We were now sure that we would get to Tokyo well before the Russian battleships were anywhere near.

Along with the other First Class passengers, we passed the night at the luxurious Hotel de la Poste, which had retained its French name even if now under the thumb of the Colonial Office. The passage through the Canal, although tedious due to the one-way-only traffic, was pleasant, and once through the Red Sea, we charged with full steam ahead eastward across the Arabian Sea to Colombo, the capital of the lovely spice island of Ceylon. Our ship pulled into port for re-provisioning, allowing us an overnight stay in the magnificent Galle Face Hotel. It had been a quarter-century since I had been in this part of the world, and now I could see why the English were so besotted with the Raj. The level of grandeur, service, dining, and elegance was beyond my imagining. It thrilled my heart to see how the British Empire had lifted this once heathen land into a veritable isle of delight.

Our stay in Ceylon was all too brief, and we departed the following afternoon, with Singapore as our next port of call. Again, we were fortunate to have sunny skies, pleasant seas with gentle swells, and winds that did not exceed ten knots. It took only two days to cross the Bay of Bengal and enter the Malacca Straits. That narrow passage is reputed to be among the most dangerous on earth, beset by shoals, and rocks, and pirates. Good luck was with us, and we were tugged into the Port of Singapore.

Once again, the First Class passengers were led off the ship and to our rooms in a splendid hotel – this time the Raffles. The docks were inundated with beggars, rickshaw drivers, and hawkers, all shouting to us regarding every known object and service imaginable, some of which had no place in the life of an English gentleman. Fortunately, the hotel had a carriage waiting, and we were soon sitting in a veritable oasis of gardens in the courtyard of the Raffles. As the sun set, we made our way to the Long Bar and ordered brandies. Instead of our drink of choice arriving in a familiar snifter, the bartender, who had introduced himself as Mr. Ngiam Tong Boon, placed in front of us tall glasses holding a cherry-colored drink and topped with a thin layer of foam.

"And what, my good man," I demanded of the barkeep, "is this?"

"Ah, gentlemen," he replied with a friendly if sly smile, "it is our own humble concoction, our recipe for a gin sling. It is more refreshing than brandy. Please, enjoy."

I imbibed. It was pleasant enough, but seemed no more than a mixture of tropical fruit juices, with a touch of gin. Being thirsty, I downed it rather quickly and requested a second and then a third. Then I stood up. Then I sat back down again. Whatever Mr. Tong Boon had put in his Singapore sling, it was not just fruit juice.

Early the following morning, I rose and made my way to one of the interior verandas on which the staff served an excellent breakfast. After several cups of coffee, I felt that my head had sufficiently cleared from the bombardment of the previous evening, and I was steady enough on my feet to venture out on to Orchard Road. I had no sooner walked into the teeming multitudes than a small man with a portable stool, and a wooden tool case accosted me.

14

As a result of that meeting, by the afternoon my feet were shod with a fine new set of shoes.

The final stretch on the P & O liner took us from Singapore to Hong Kong. This time, the travel agent had booked us into the Peak Hotel at the top of the funicular railway. From our balcony, the view of Hong Kong Harbor, with endless Chinese Junks, freighters, and the fleet of Star Ferries coming and going, was a sight to behold. That evening, having learned my lesson in Singapore, I drank nothing but tea. The following morning I descended the Peak Tram to Queen's Road, quite confident that I would not squander any more of my funds on articles of fashion that I simply did not need. However, while I was peacefully strolling along the street, a gentleman of the Indian race came out of his shop and stopped me on the pavement.

The following morning I not only had a suit tailored exactly for my body but five new shirts to go with it.

By the time I had boarded our new ship, the Moji-Maru of the Japan Mail Steamship Line, I was better dressed and shod than I had been in my entire life.

Now our final destination would be Yokohama, the sprawling harbor city south of Tokyo where ships from all over the world were loading and unloading, bringing in coal and petroleum and taking away all sorts of manufactured goods and endless packing cases filled with exquisite and very expensive Japanese silk.

It was during this last segment of our sea journey that Holmes finally sat me down and expounded on what theories he had formed from the hundreds of pages of data he had read and re-read.

"It is always," he said, and I knew what was coming, "a serious risk to form theories, let alone conclusions before having all possible data in front of one. Nevertheless, such evidence as has been given to me, and it is quite extensive, is pointing suspiciously to the upstanding Christian missionary wife of our Envoy. The only possible conclusion is that she is leading a very curious double life.

She is not behaving in a manner that is loyal to the Empire, and I daresay, not even a manner appropriate to a Christian wife."

"Really, Holmes, explain how it is possible for anyone to have data, as you call it, on the private affairs of a respected American woman? What sort of Peeping Toms are we dealing with?"

"Oh, my dear doctor. Did you not listen when Mycroft explained that there is no such thing as a diplomat who is not a spy? Else, why would we pay them? The Ministers Resident in every legation, embassy or high commission are expected to report on the Envoy. The Chargés d'Affaires inform on the Ministers and on down the line. The attachés inform on their superiors, and all those who are not protected by diplomatic immunity, all those drivers and chefs and secretaries, inform on everyone. How else would we keep them honest? They are all quite brilliant and energetic young Englishmen, and Lord only knows—and I would not be surprised if even He blushes from time to time—what mischief they could get themselves up to when they are ten thousand miles away from home. Why, if they thought they could get away with yielding to all manner of heathen temptations, every Embassy and High Commission in the Empire would crumble."

"Even if," I queried, "they were much happier places? Ah, not necessary to answer that one, Holmes. Back to our righteous Christian missionary lady, now the esteemed wife of His Excellency, our Envoy. What evidence is there that leads you to cast aspersions on her honor?"

For the next hour, he delivered a monologue consisting of a long list of small actions that had been observed, and that could not be fully explained. However, he saved the most damning items for the last.

"Once and sometimes even twice a week, she sends off letters, written partially in indecipherable code, and partially in Russian, to an agent of the Czar who is using his appointment as an instructor in mathematics as his cover."

"Do not the Japanese have their own math teachers?" I challenged. "These Oriental chaps are all supposed to be inhumanly talented in arithmetic."

"He is teaching at the School for Girls run by the Society of Friends."

"Ah ha, the peaceful Quakers imparting good manners and the Christian gospel, or at least their version of it, to obedient young Japanese women. A perfect cover indeed for a Russian spy."

Chapter Three   Have a Lovely Hanami

t was the twenty-eighth of March when we arrived in port. The journey had taken just over three weeks. The Russian Fleet was reported to still be somewhere in the Indian Ocean, not having yet entered the Malacca Straits. The Japanese were already in control of Port Arthur on the Chinese mainland, having invaded back in February, and had recently taken over more and more slices of Manchuria. The Russians were not at all happy, and whatever might happen next, anywhere in the world, was beyond imagining.

A couple of tugs brought us into one of the piers in Yokohama. I had fully expected that we would again be mobbed with beggars and hawkers and the like as soon as we set foot on shore. To my surprise, there was not one to be seen. The massive port facilities were scrupulously clean. I did not see a scrap of litter anywhere, not a single pallet or packing case that was not lined up in perfect order. There was not a trace of the mayhem I was used to at Southampton or Liverpool. Everything was moving decently and in order.

As we descended the gangplank, I heard our names being called. A well-dressed young man was waving at us and beckoning us in his direction. We walked over to him, and the first thing that struck me was the quality of his attire. His beautifully tailored, quiet suit spoke of bespoke on Saville Row and not merely an imitation from Hong Kong. Nearly hidden, but exposed just enough to be noticed, was a set of gold cufflinks in which rather large emeralds were set. His silk cravat was set off by a diamond tie pin. Whoever this young chap was, he was definitely from the upper classes of Nippon.

As we approached him, he bowed deeply and held that position for a full five seconds. When his back was unbent, he flashed a broad, gleaming smile.

"Sherlock-san, and Dr. John-san, it is my honor to welcome such esteemed men to my country. I have been sent to make sure that your stay here in Nippon is one of the greatest pleasure and enlightenment. My name is Toshitikitimbonosorimbo. But my Japanese friends all call me Toshi, and my English friends call me Tommy. So please, gentlemen, Tommy, at your service."

His English bore a slight Oriental accent but was otherwise flawless, right down to the articles. I was about to say something appropriately gracious in reply when Holmes brusquely answered back.

"Who sent you?"

"Ah, of course, how poor on my part not to inform you, Sherlock-san. Because you are so famous all over the world, and because the Emperor Himself is a fan of your stories, I have been sent by the office of our Prime Minister."

"You don't say. Where did you learn to speak English?"

He bowed again and smiled. "I learned first from my teachers, but I have just returned from two years in your beautiful country."

"What were you doing there?"

"One of your wealthy countrymen, a Mr. Cecil Rhodes, left some money in his estate so that promising young men from all over the world could come and study at Oxford. Although there were many men who were more worthy than I, this honor was given to me."

"The Japanese," said Sherlock, "are not eligible for Rhodes scholarships."

"That is true, Sherlock-san, but I was also honored to be made a citizen of Australia and so became eligible."

An honor indeed, I thought. The program for Rhodes Scholars had only started two years ago. It was the most prestigious scholarship on offer anywhere in the Empire, or in the entire world for that matter. The competition had been intense. If our Tommy had won one of the coveted places, he must be quite the sharp young lad.

"Please, Sherlock-san and John-san, follow me. A Pullman car is waiting at the station to take you into Tokyo. Your luggage will be looked after and will arrive in your rooms in the Imperial Hotel. Please, this way."

His manners and bearing were carelessly aristocratic. He was several yards in front of us, and I could not help but notice that dockhands, bureaucrats, and even soldiers bowed slightly to him and stepped back so that we could pass.

"My," I whispered to Holmes. "Quite the impressive young chap."

"He's a spy."

We quickly cleared the docks and entered a stretch of well-tended gardens that ran along the side of a wide boulevard. We have pleasant places like this in England, of course, but what caused me to stop in my tracks and gasp in wonder was the enormous mass of white and pinkish blossoms with which the trees were laden. For at least fifty yards, we walked under a veritable tunnel of blossoms through which the sunlight was dappling the pavement. Petals fluttered down on top of us as we passed. Under many of the spreading branches, small gatherings of Japanese people were sitting on the ground with picnic lunches being shared amongst them. Some were elderly couples or clusters of aging friends; others were family;

still others were young men and a few young women who I presumed were students or office workers. All seemed other-worldly happy and enjoying the ethereal atmosphere.

Tommy observed my staring and explained. "It is *Hanami* time. For only two or three weeks every spring, the cherry blossoms appear, and it is one of our favorite customs to walk or sit together and let the experience of the blossoms overtake us. Please, doctor, allow your mind to be released and enter into it as well."

Holmes leaned over and whispered to me. "You will do no such thing, Watson. The last thing I need is having you say good-bye to your brain within minutes of getting off the boat. I need you to be fully rationale. Kindly remember that."

Very well, I thought, be a spoilsport, Holmes. I could do my *Hanami* by myself.

It was not a long walk from the pier to the train station, and we were soon passing through a building that, with its small dark shuttered windows and wide expanses of whitewashed walls, looked more like it belonged on a military base

Tommy led us to a siding where a gleaming Pullman car was waiting for us. The interior rivaled any parlor or club room I had visited in England, all fine leather and polished furniture. A dark-skinned porter in a white jacket soon appeared and offered us refreshments. Within ten minutes, I could hear the car being coupled to another and felt the jolt as we began our journey.

We had no sooner begun to move than Tommy initiated a friendly inquisition of Holmes. He was clearly familiar with every detail of every story I had published. He quizzed Holmes, affecting the manner of an idolizing schoolboy. Holmes smiled and replied to his increasingly prying questions by appearing to give sincere, forthcoming answers while revealing nothing that had not already been told in the press or in *The Strand*. I found the dance of two sharp intellects to be utterly intriguing.

Half-an-hour later we stopped, and Tommy announced that we had arrived at Tokyo Central Station. Porters appeared as if from nowhere and carried our baggage to the *Marunouchi* side of the station, and then Tommy led us the few blocks to the Imperial Hotel and checked us in. Holmes and I shared a suite of splendidly furnished rooms, and, after so many weeks of sleeping in a ship's cabin, I was rather looking forward to a nap on the plush English bed, covered with thick, crisp Irish linens. With some difficulty, eventually reduced to bluntness, we shooed Tommy away and stretched out in our respective rooms. I enjoyed no more than the allotted forty winks when there was a knock on the door. I opened it, and a large young blond chap in the uniform of the Royal Marines was standing there, holding a diplomatic case. I invited the fellow in and bade him relax. He graciously refused and remained at attention. Holmes emerged, greeted the young man, and in a friendly manner, inquired of his name and home county.

"Yes, sir. My name is Archibald Levenworth, sir. From North Yorkshire, sir. I am terribly sorry to disturb you, Mr. Holmes, but I have to have you sign for this case. Would you mind, please, sir?"

"Of course not, Archie. What is it they say about Yorkshire? Ah, yes. You can always tell a Yorkshire man, but you can't tell him much. That true, Archie?"

The big fellow broke into a grin. "Sir, I can only speak for my dear father and grandfather, who have spent their entire lives there, sir. And on their behalf, sir, yes, it is absolutely true."

Holmes and I laughed, and he signed the form and bid our good-day to the strapping Marine. But both of us sensed that he was not eager to be off.

"Is there something else, my good man?" inquired Holmes.

"Well, sir, it is a bit embarrassing, but when I told my mates I was taking a case over to you, they all demanded that I have you and Dr. Watson sign their copies of *The Strand* or else they would give me what for when I returned. Would you mind, terribly, sir?"

"Of course, not," said Holmes. From his satchel, Archie produced a stack of magazines and Holmes, and I dutifully signed each of them on the page where my latest story was printed.

"Really," said Holmes, "have you boys nothing else to do while guarding the Embassy but sit around and read sensationalized stories in magazines?"

"Well, sir, it is, you might say, a bit of all right, meaning that we get to stay in comfortable barracks and eat good food, and are never in danger. But we were all trained very hard, sir, to fight for God and King Edward, and frankly, sir, it's deadly boring."

"Then may I wish you a nice gunfight someday soon," said Holmes, giving the lad a clap on his shoulder and sending him on his way.

"Ah, yes, Watson," he continued. "Let me see what we have here. What do you suppose my dear older brother has sent to us? Ah, ha. Just as I thought, a kindly telegram welcoming us to Japan. Here, read it."

I did. It ran:

YOU HAVE HAD OVER THREE WEEKS TO LAZE AROUND. I NEED YOU TO GET TO WORK IMMEDIATELY, SHERLOCK. FIND OUT WHAT HAPPENED TO THE AMERICAN CHAP. WE NEED TO HAVE THE YANKS OWE US ONE. START BY TALKING TO THEIR SECOND SECRETARY, SMATHERS. HE IS OUR MAN IN THEIR LEGATION. REPORT BACK TO ME BY FRIDAY.   MYCROFT.

"Just as I expected. Very well, then, my good doctor. Your nap has been unkindly cut short, and we shall read the files on the Deputy Head of the American Mission who, if I recall, was not a good swimmer."

Chapter Four   The Drowned American

He opened the case, extracted one of the files, and began to read, passing each page to me when he had finished it.

The Deputy at the US Legation, a fellow named Julian Boulanger, hailed from somewhere in Maine and, with all odds against him, had graduated from Georgetown University in the nation's capital with a degree in law. He had entered the Foreign Service upon receiving his degree and had served in Reykjavik, Ottawa, Stockholm, and Moscow, working his way up the diplomatic ladder with each move. He arrived in Japan in 1903 and, as he had learned to speak Russian while in Moscow, he was particularly adroit at dealing with the Russians before they were forced to vacate.

One morning just over a month ago, he failed to show up for work. For several days, no one knew what had happened to him. Then a fisherman pulled his body out from under a pier on the Sumida River, not far from the Tsukiji Fish Market. It should have become a major issue between the Japanese and the Americans, but it never made the press in New York beyond a short paragraph bemoaning the tragic death of an American overseas by drowning while out for a swim.

The American Legation was in the Akasaka neighborhood of Tokyo, just south of the Diet and government ministry buildings.

Holmes sent a note off to a Mr. Godfrey Smathers and had a very quick reply requesting that we come and see him in the morning.

"If we depart at an early hour," suggested Holmes, "our eager young Rhodes scholar will not follow us. I suggest that we retire and give the poor boy cause for some minor distress."

The following morning, very early, Secretary Smathers met us in a small *izakaya* not far from the US Legation. He was dressed in an American style business suit and was leaning against the backrest of the padded bench with a cigarette in one hand, and a glass of what I assumed was *sake* in the other. A brown wide-awake hat was on the bench beside him.

"Well, if it ain't the famous Sherlock Holmes and Dr. Watson. Let me guess; first time in Japan? Maybe even the first time working with diligent, devoted spies. Ah, yes. I can see it is by just looking at you two. Well, set yourselves down and have a drink. Once you acquire a taste for this sake concoction, it can become quite palatable. Let me pour you both one."

He did not get up out of his seat to greet us, and neither did he offer a handshake. He reached for the large bottle that was sitting beside him and poured two small glasses until they overflowed into the small dish in which they rested.

"So," he continued, after raising his glass to us, "is it true that Sherlock Holmes is really the little brother of great-and-powerful Sir Mycroft. Who would of guessed?"

"And good morning to you as well, Mr. Smathers," replied Holmes. "I believe that my familial relations are of no consequence to our meeting. I have been requested by His Majesty's government to investigate the apparent murder of your Resident Minister, and I believe that you are being paid by His Majesty to assist me. Is that not correct, sir?"

Smathers smirked and scornfully repeated Holmes's words. "Oh, jolly good, '*Is that not correct, sir?*' Yes, jolly good indeed. Yeah, Holmes, I'm getting paid by your pompous big brother to help you, so help you, I will. Here's all I know. Our American security boys, who are bloody good at their jobs even if you snotty Brits like to think otherwise, did a full investigation after we found our diplomat floating in the river. It turns out that our dear Julian, who had risen to second-in-command in this post, had a few unsavory habits that led him into places he should not have been. Every minute of his last week on earth was tracked down, and our boy spent a few too many of them in the company of a lovely *geisha*. One of the loveliest in all of Tokyo, in fact. And since she was so lovely, she was also the prize belonging of a General Ishiwara, who had a reputation for being one very tough SOB who did not like sharing his toys. And arrogant little Julian, who thought he was the smartest fellow at the post, got himself caught *in flagrante delicto* and was duly dealt with in such a manner, it was obvious, as to be a lesson to any other American, or Brit for that matter if they were capable of it, who might be making eyes at a local geisha. And that, Mr. Holmes, is what happened. Kind of delicate, right? So are you surprised that we did not want it splashed all over the press?"

"Not surprising at all," replied Holmes in a friendly tone. "But, my dear chap, you know what a nasty old bear my brother can be. And if that is all I can put in my report, I will have my head bitten quite off. So I must ask you to do me the favor of allowing me to inspect your Mr. Boulanger's residence and belongings and at least make it look as if I did my homework. Would you mind terribly making that arrangement for me?"

I sensed that Holmes knew right well that his polite request of Smathers could not be refused if the American wished to remain in the good graces of Mycroft and, more important, retain his generous stipend from London. Smathers glared at Holmes but held his tongue, eventually nodding his compliance.

"Follow me," he said. He rose, paid the tab for the sake, and walked out onto the street. We followed at a short distance until he came to a gate leading into what I assumed was a diplomatic compound for foreigners. There were two guards at the gate, dressed in the uniform of the United States Marines, and Smathers spoke to them briefly, whereupon one of them searched through a cabinet in the guardhouse and handed a set of keys to our American guide.

"In years gone by," he said, "they used to make all of us foreigners live in the Tsukiji settlement beside the river. But they needed that space for their fish market, so now we get to roam the city, more or less. Julian's residence is up ahead. He was fairly high up on the ladder, so he was provided with better housing. It hasn't been cleaned out since he died. They're all still waiting for someone from his family to come and take away his belongings. Our boys went through everything and found nothing more than what I've already told you. So if you want to snoop around for the rest of the day, go ahead. Just leave the keys with the guards when you go. And since I have better things to do, I will dump you guys here. I will be at the American Legation if you need me again."

He opened the door of a pleasant villa, handed Holmes the ring of keys, and departed.

The residence was spacious and well-furnished with western furniture. The Japanese style of rooms with sliding doors that opened on to a garden had been adapted, and it made for a very attractive place in which to live. After a cursory tour of the lodgings, Holmes sat himself in one of the plush sofas and turned to me. I knew what was coming.

"Very well, my dear doctor, what did you make of Smathers's account of the American's demise?"

For years he had been asking me questions like this, and no matter how much I sought to reason and observe, I was never able to come up with sufficient correct deductions. However, Holmes never stopped asking, and I never stopped trying.

"The story," I ventured, "about the geisha did not strike me as reliable."

"Ah ha! I agree, and pray tell, why not?"

"I only know what I have read, but I had three weeks on board ship to do nothing but read books about Japan, including a quite fascinating one. *The World of Flower and Willow* was the title, but I cannot remember the author's name, except that it was a Scottish woman. She said that geishas were not treated like a wife or daughter, or even a mistress. They were independent women with highly trained artistic, musical, and conversational skills. They were free to spend time with whomsoever they wished once they had passed into the ranks of the full-fledged geisha. So, the idea that a man of means and reputation would kill another man in a jealous rage over a geisha is just not something that would take place in Japan. I believe, if I remember correctly, that their aristocrats and generals and the like would often send their favorite geisha and pay her fee, as a present to someone they wished to impress or thank. That is about all I remember from my reading. Unfortunately, that book is on board the S.S. Delhi and on its way back to London. But what about you, Holmes?"

"I agree entirely, my dear friend, and have nothing to add."

This was a most unusual response to my efforts, and I was more than somewhat pleased with myself. Feeling confident, I kept going.

"I cannot imagine that Smathers, who is Mycroft's man in the American Embassy, would be knowingly deceiving us with his story, since if found out he would lose his stipend from your brother. Therefore, there is most likely some element of truth to his account, but no doubt somewhat confused."

"Brilliant, Watson. You're doing splendidly. Keep going."

"This chap, Mr. Boulanger, had rather costly tastes and habits. The cabinet is full of fine liquor. The suits in his wardrobe are of a select quality, and the pieces of art on his walls would not, I surmise, be issued by his employer. This fellow either came from money or had a need for it in order to cover his habits."

"Well done, Watson! Well done, indeed. Now, take the data you have acquired and your deductions and form a theory concerning the crime. We already know how he died, but who might have done it and, most critically, *why*."

I had been feeling a bit chuffed but knew that I was now on shakier ground. Nevertheless, I soldiered on.

"Very well, Holmes, I will give it a try. A man might kill another man for private reasons related to jealousy, or vengeance, or a fear of being exposed. Sensible men do not kill other men who owe them gambling debts, since a gambler who owes you money but is still alive is worth far more than one who owes you but is dead. Or, it could be for reasons of state, such as treason, or fear of treason."

"Exactly, now keep it up, old boy."

"If his personal needs were being attended to by a geisha of the upper ranks, then it is not likely that Mr. Boulanger would be involved in any indecent friendships with any other women, so we can tentatively rule out jealous husbands or competing suitors."

"Indeed, we can. Pray, continue."

"If a high-ranking Japanese general truly did have a hand in his murder, then I would be inclined to think it related more to matters of state, to international intrigue, treason, and the like."

"As would I, Watson. And, as we are dealing with diplomats, who Mycroft assures us are all spies to the last man, then it is to that probable field of affairs that we must now devote our attention. Allow me then to suggest that we go through this residence with a fine-tooth comb looking for anything that might give us a clue as to what the fuss was over."

I nodded my consent. We had no other meeting scheduled for the morning, and while searching through the effects of a dead man was not a particularly dignified task, it went with the job of solving a crime.

"Where shall I begin, Holmes?"

He gazed around the room, pondering his response, and then settled his eye on the bookcase.

"I will begin with his desk and files, and you, my dear doctor, with his books."

Mr. Boulanger's books were neatly arranged on a large bookcase, with the fictional literature clearly separated from the non-fiction. There must have been over one hundred novels and a score of collections of poetry. All were in order by the last name of the author, and I began, therefore, with *A*. One by one, I pulled the books off the shelf, checked the small hidden place in the bookcase behind them, and held them by their spines to see if anything would fall out. That was followed by a quick inspection of the endpapers and flyleaves. In a few minutes, I had disposed of Henry Adams, Conrad Aiken, Louisa May Alcott, Horatio Alger and Jane Austin but had found nothing. And so it went through the letter *B,* and then on into *C*. I was strongly tempted to stop and read some passages from books that I had heard of but had never had the opportunity to enjoy, but they would have to wait for there was an entire half a shelf of James Fennimore Cooper. First came *The Spy,* then *The Pioneers, The Pilot,* and *The Last of the Mohicans,* but then, oddly, a second copy of *The Spy.* I held it open like I did all the others, and nothing fell out, but a flipping of the pages caused me to sputter for my companion.

"Holmes! Here. Look at this!"

There was not a single word of printed text inside the volume. It was lined in the manner of a ledger book with the back portion blank, but the front half of the pages entirely filled with notes and numbers. I handed it to Holmes. He took it, sat down on one of the sofas, and began to read the pages slowly. For the first few minutes, his gaze was devoted to the opening pages, then with a slight jerk of his head and a trace of a smile, he flipped to the last page on which an entry had been made. The trace of a smile slowly broadened until he was positively grinning.

"Out with it, Holmes," I ordered. "What have you found?"

For the next minute, he did not respond. He just kept on smiling and muttering "Ah ha" and nodding his head. Then his countenance suddenly clouded over, and I heard and quiet, "Uh oh. Oh dear."

"My dear doctor," he said, looking up at me, "do take a look at what our dead American spy has left us." He turned the book in my direction and held it open so I could read. On the final page of entries I read, in a neat script:

January 15, 1905

Received from Ottawa. 2000 Ross. Remitted $10,000 in gold to Le Blanc.

Paid to cartage $1000.

Received from Nippon. $20,000.

Western Union transfer to Kidder, Peabody. $9000.

On the preceding page, was a similar entry but with somewhat more detail.

December 30, 1904

Received from Ottawa: 1000 Ross. Remitted $5,000 in gold to Le Blanc for payment to Gen. Federov.

Paid for cartage and brokerage services: $500.

Received from Nippon via Ishiwara: $10,000.

Western Union transfer to Kidder, Peabody: $4500.

The earlier entries were all of the same order. Articles identified only by an unrecognized name appear to have been imported from Canada, Argentina, Great Britain, Germany, and numerous other countries. They were then sold on to various entities that had Japanese names. Many different names from numerous countries of origin were noted with some recurring often and others only once or twice.

"What, Holmes, do you make of this?"

"Obviously, our man was doing what any honest spy does to supplement his income. He was using his diplomatic status to import goods into Japan and sell them at a considerable profit. His account with Kidder Peabody and Company must be quite rich. Carrying on like this is generally not approved of by any Foreign Office of any country, but the prohibition is honored in the breach all over the world. There is nothing untoward about that. But one of the names of his co-conspirators gave me pause."

"Might that have been *General Federov?*"

"It might."

For the next two hours, we pored over the ledger book and continued to search Mr. Boulanger's villa. We had hoped to find some of whatever it was he was importing into Japan, but there was nothing of the sort to be found.

"He must," I asserted, "be using another warehouse somewhere. Heaven only knows how we could find it."

"Heaven? Perhaps. Or maybe those who think they belong there."

I could not understand what he was saying, and then, of all things, he began to sing:

> *If the Army and the Navy*
> *Ever look on Heaven's scenes,*
> *They will find the streets are guarded*
> *By United States Marines.*

"You do not," he said with a friendly, howbeit condescending smile, "appear to be familiar with the Hymn of the United States Marines."

I had never heard of it.

"Well then, it occurred to me that if shipments of anything were coming and coming from this compound, the young chaps at the gate must have seen something."

We walked back to the gate of the compound, and Holmes approached the two strapping lads who stood by the guardhouse.

"Terribly sorry to bother you lads, but is it possible that you know who I am?"

One of them looked at him, a little perplexed and replied.

"Sir! We know that you are Mr. Sherlock Holmes, Sir! And the gentleman with you is Dr. Watson, Sir!"

"Ah, I thought you might, and if it is not against your orders, may I request that you stand at ease and speak freely?"

The two fellows looked at each other, gave shy smiles, and stood at ease.

"Welcome, Mr. Holmes. Sure we know who you are. We've read all your stories that Dr. Watson writes. We sort of can't wait to get back to the barracks and tell the rest of our unit about meeting you. Most exciting thing that's happened this week, sir."

"And, if you will forgive my curiosity, have you any idea why I am here? I assure you that whatever you say will never be repeated."

One chap instinctively shook his head, although his wide eyes betrayed his answer. The other gave a shrug and replied.

"Well sir, I'm not wanting to look like a bonehead, so I'd have to say it must have something to do with them finding that stiff in the drink, Mr. Boulanger, that is. Somebody done him in, and it's all hush-hush. So you being a hawkshaw and all, we figured that the brass must have called in reinforcements. That's just what we kind of guess, sir."

"And right you are. Now, would I be correct if I were to guess that you two lads wouldn't mind helping me to solve the mystery of the murder of Mr. Boulanger?"

All pretense of being on guard disappeared from the faces of the lads, and they began to beam like schoolboys just let out early.

"Oh, boy! We would love to do that, wouldn't we, Jimmy. That would be a real humdinger for us, sir. But you just can't put our names in any story. If our Captain hears about it, we'll be called on the carpet and given the third degree. What can we do, sir?"

"Very good. Well then, Marines, the mystery is this. I have evidence that Mr. Boulanger received and sent many different shipments of goods, but there is not a scrap of them to be found in his villa. Have you seen anything coming and going over the past few months?"

The chap who had been addressed as Jimmy came over and stood close to Holmes and me. In a quiet voice, he said, "There were livery wagons arriving at least once a week, loaded with goods. And other wagons come in empty and leave loaded. It was going on real regular up until he got knocked off. But because all these men who are the uppity-ups at the Legation have diplomatic immunity, we are not supposed to write anything down. But all of us on this detail saw it all the time. Real regular, sir."

"You don't say. Were the wagons marked in any way? Could you tell where they were coming from?"

"They came from the docks, sir. The cases and barrels all have the name of the ship they came on stenciled on their sides. During the past few months, a lot was coming from Canada. Had the *Empress of Japan* marked on the shipments. That's the ship that sails from Vancouver, sir. And the wagons that took stuff away, sir, they belonged to the Japs, sir. To their military, sir."

"Ah, very interesting, my boy," said Holmes. "But if they were not taken to the villa, where did they go?"

"Well, Mr. Holmes, all the men here, and all the families, have a space over in the warehouse, off beyond the houses, sir. That's where they store all their barrels and packing cases. That's how these folks get moved from place to place, sir. Everything they own, and I mean *everything,* gets put in barrels and cases every few years and they move on to their next post, so they all keep their barrels and cases, sir, and guard them real tight."

"How very reasonable," Holmes assented. "Would it be possible for you to take us to the warehouse?"

Chapter Five   In the Warehouse

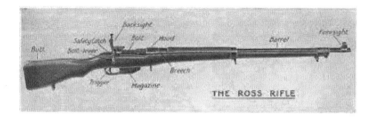

THE ROSS RIFLE

A look of confusion spread over the marine's face. "Oh, sir. We can't leave our post. The Captain would read the riot act if he ever heard we did that. We would love to be able to help, sir, but that would get us tossed in the hoosegow for sure. Sorry, sir."

Holmes smiled at them. "Of course. You are fine soldiers, and you should never leave your post when there is no apparent reason to do so."

Then he jumped around and pointed to the houses and shouted. "Oh! Did you hear that? There was a gunshot over there. You heard that didn't you, Watson?"

I knew my lines.

"Yes! Yes! It was a gunshot. Oh! There's a second one. It's coming from beyond the houses. Marines, somebody may be in trouble. You have to investigate immediately. It could be a matter of life and death!"

At first, the two fellows looked dumbfounded, and then grins spread across their faces.

Jimmy responded loudly. "Oh, my. Sherlock Holmes and Dr. Watson report hearing gunshots, Gerry. We better get over there. Somebody could be in trouble. C'mon! On the double."

They took off at a run, and we followed them, walking. Behind the lanes of residences stood a featureless building, and our two Marines were standing in front of it, smiling, with the door wide open.

"Do you think the shots came from inside, Mr. Holmes?"

"I am certain of it," Holmes replied, stifling a laugh.

"Right, sir. Then we'll just have to look."

The two Marines entered the warehouse and led us to a door along one of the hallways.

"I believe that this is where you heard the shots coming from, Mr. Holmes," said Jimmy. "Now, sir, we could knock the door down, but it might be a lot easier if you would take the keys that Mr. Smathers left with you. Odds are, sir, one of them is going to let us in."

I had the keys in my pocket and tried several of them on the door until the lock shifted, and the door opened. Stepping inside, we could see what I estimated to be a hundred or more wooden cases stacked from floor to ceiling. All were about six feet in length and all stamped with the name of *Empress of Japan – Canadian Pacific*.

Holmes leaned his head down toward the closest case and announced, "I do believe that I heard someone shouting for help inside that case. His life may be in danger. Marine, could you please help me rescue him."

Gerry moved forward, raised his rifle in the air and brought the butt end smashing down on the padlock. It flew off the side of the case and onto the floor. The two marines then each pried the top up with their bayonets and flung it open.

"Wow!" burst Jimmy. "Isn't that just a lollapalooza! Those rifles are brand spanking new."

The entire crate was filled with military rifles, all gleaming and waiting their first use. Jimmy lifted one out and, with a practiced hand, slid the bolt back and forth in its place.

"It's a Ross," he said. "The new Canadian gun. Best sniper rifle in the world, but useless in battle."

"How is it you know this gun?" asked Holmes, somewhat incredulously.

"We're Marines, sir. We like guns. They're sort of our hobby. When we come together for a bit of a bash, we talk about girls and guns and baseball, and grouse about the food. Arguing about which rifle is better is just one of the things we do, sir. We Marines are issued Springfields, and the Limeys get Lee-Enfields. But starting last year, the Canucks started using these here Ross Rifles. Looks like there are maybe twenty of them in this here case. Must be a thousand or more in the room here. You're the detective sir, but I'd bet that our Mr. Boulanger was bringing these in and then selling them to the Japs."

He handed the rifle over to his fellow Marine and picked up a second. Gerry similarly shuttled the bolt back and forth and raised the rifle to his shoulder and sighted it at some unknown enemy. Then slowly, he brought it back down and raised the lock section to just below his eyes and stared at it intently.

"Something's wrong here, Jimmy."

"What's wrong?"

"This thing is a piece of junk. It's the Ross design, all right, but look. That bolt hasn't been decently polished. The sights aren't lined up properly. The varnish looks like it's been painted on by a five-year-old. The Canadian soldiers don't like this gun, but I've never heard them say that it looks cheap. The ones I've held before are beautifully finished. This one is rubbish."

He handed it on to me, reached into the case, and brought out another gun that he handed to Holmes. It had been over twenty-five years since I had held a military rifle in my hands, but I could still tell the difference between a finely crafted weapon and cheap imitation. What I was holding was the latter.

Holmes looked over the rifle in his hands. He put it back in the box and took out a second one. A curious look that I had seen appear many times over the years came across his face.

"These guns have serial numbers stamped on the plate just above the trigger."

"They do," said Gerry. "All our guns have those now."

"Is it normal," asked Holmes, "for every gun to have the identical serial number?"

"What!" sputtered Gerry. He grabbed another gun from the case, and then another. "Jeepers creepers! They're all the same. Every one of them. That's right goopy. What nut made these?"

Together we pulled out and examined the rifles remaining in the case. All showed the same sloppy degree of manufacture, and all bore the same serial numbers. We put the guns back, and Holmes turned to the two Marines.

"Gentlemen, again, I ask you to help me solve a mystery. You know the world of weapons far better than I. If I wanted someone to copy a rifle design and provide cheap imitations, where would I go to have that done."

The two of them looked at each other and then in unison replied, "Russia."

They then provided several anecdotes giving additional examples of grenades, petards, artillery shells and the like that had been discovered to have been made in Russia and sold as if they had been made by Mauser or Remington. Holmes thanked then for their help and promised that their assistance would remain a confidential matter. (Reader: Please note that the names I have given them are not their true names).

"Very well, Watson," said Holmes as we walked away from the compound in search of a cab, "your further deductions."

"Now Holmes, you know it is never wise to form conclusions before you have sufficient data."

He laughed at the tease and, emboldened, I continued.

"It would appear that our dead American was running a very profitable and utterly dishonest business of importing arms from Russia, but shipping them through Canada, and then selling them to the Japanese Military, pretending that they came from Canada."

"That is a reasonable conclusion, given the data at hand."

"If I were the chap in the Japanese Army that was buying them from him, and discovered that not only was I being sold a pig in a poke but that the money was going to the country with whom I was at war, I would imagine that I might not be a very happy fellow."

"Unhappy enough to have the man who had been robbing you murdered?"

"Oh, yes, I think so. These Oriental fellows are terribly big on not having their honor besmirched, and if I were the General who was exposed as giving the Emperor's money to a Yankee swindler, I might add in a spot of torture as well."

"I agree, Watson. And do you recall the Russian supplier's name?"

"Yes. Federov."

Chapter Six   The Very Second Minister

We found our way back to the hotel. The Japanese cab driver did not need my efforts from the list of useful phrases. He took one look at us and said, "Ah …. Imperio Hotel-o?"

As we entered the lobby, Tommy was waiting for us. He leapt up from his chair and rushed over to us.

"Sherlock-san, and Dr. John-san, where have you been? It is not safe for you to wander around Tokyo by yourself. There are many places where foreigners can be robbed. Please, gentlemen, our government is very concerned for your safety. You must not go out like that again without me."

"Oh, dear," said Holmes with feigned concern. "We went out to admire the blossoms. Had a lovely walk around the palace grounds. The cherry trees were quite splendid. I do not remember feeling unsafe at all. But I do thank you for your concern."

Tommy was visibly upset. While he continued to bow and express concern for our well-being, I noticed that his fists were clenched and perceived that he more than a little angry with us.

"Gentlemen," he said. "It is good that you have returned. An appointment has been arranged for you with your Legation in two hours from now. Your Second Minister wishes to meet with you to discuss the lecture tour of Mr. Holmes. I will wait for you here. May I ask you please to meet me here at one o'clock?"

"Of course, we shall do that," said Holmes, cheerily. Holmes bowed to Tommy and turned and headed for the staircase.

I immediately began to write up our report on the day's activities while Holmes read through the latest batch of cables and documents that had arrived from Mycroft. By just before one o'clock, I had it finished. Holmes and I went over the final version, and we sent it off to the British Legation, to the attention of our Mr. Grant Munro, the Envoy Extraordinary and Minister Plenipotentiary.

The British Legation was housed in a large red brick complex just across the moat from the north side of the Imperial Palace grounds. We entered through the large iron gates and into the graveled courtyard. A polished carriage stood at the entrance to the buildings and, as we were approaching it, a man and a woman emerged from the doorway and walked toward it. She had her arm through his, and they appeared to be chatting pleasantly. Both were elegantly dressed, but what struck me immediately was their stature. The man was broad-shouldered, slender, and considerably taller than Holmes. The woman, however, was as tall as he, although I noticed (as a result of years of tutoring by Holmes) that her boots accounted for an inch or two. She was not wearing her hair on the top of her head, as would be expected, but let her long black tresses down on her shoulders where they were bouncing gaily as she walked. Clearly, she must be an American.

"Holmes, do you suppose those two might be who I think they are?"

"Precisely. The gentleman is the Envoy and the lovely woman, according to the data we have received so far, is most likely our duplicitous villain. And a very intriguing set they are."

The carriage departed without its occupants taking notice of us, and we entered the Legation building. An attendant met us and escorted us to the office of the Second Minister.

"Ah, Mr. Sherlock Holmes and Dr. Watson," said the man with whom we had our appointment. "Delighted to have you here in Japan. I am Redvers Humphrey, the Second Minister, the one who has been given the honor of overseeing your lecture tour and giving all of your adoring fans the opportunity to see their favorite detective in the flesh. Please, gentlemen. Be seated. I am sure you are most eager to hear what I have to tell you."

He then turned to Tommy, who had followed us into his office, gave him a shallow bow, and said, "Thank you, my good man. Kindly wait in the hall. If you require anything, a cup of tea perhaps, one of our girls will be most happy to oblige."

Tommy did not look as if he wanted any of being dismissed. He bowed deeply and responded.

"Honorable Minister, sir. As the tour of Mr. Holmes and Dr. Watson is a cultural project arranged cooperatively between our two countries, it is important that I be part of this meeting, on behalf of our government, sir." He bowed again.

"Sorry, old sport," replied Humphrey. "This is just a meeting between a couple of British citizens with the British Legation. But do assure your lads over in the Diet that a report will be sent to them by tomorrow evening. Thank you, my good man. That will be all." He gestured toward the door with his arm.

Tommy did not move. Again he bowed deeply. "This will be very difficult, Mr. Minister, sir. But as the representative of the government of Japan, I am required to be present."

"No, old chap. I'm afraid to say that you are not. The authority of the Government of Japan stopped once you entered the grounds of the Legation of Great Britain. Did not anybody tell you that? Oh dear. They really must get up to snuff over there at the Diet. But please, old chap, do relax and have a cup of tea. We shan't keep you long."

Again, Tommy bowed, and again I could see that he was not at all happy. He said no more and left the room. The Minister closed the door behind him.

"They really do wish to be oh-so-very-helpful. Lovely chaps. But I'm afraid that we have to cover some items that are more sensitive than your tour. However, gentlemen, let us address the official reason for your visit to Japan—your cultural exchange on behalf of His Majesty's Government. What all will this tour entail, you ask? I can answer that question for you quite directly."

"Oh, yes, please do," said Holmes.

"Of course, happy to oblige. Where all shall we be sending you? I am sure you are dying to know."

"Yes, just dying."

"Indeed. Of course, most of your lectures will be given in and around Tokyo and Yokohama since these are the most ... the most ... the most *cosmopolitan* shall we say, of the cities of Japan. I am sure you would agree."

"I'm sure."

"But, of course, we are very aware that you have quite the assortment of followers in other cities. You are aware of that, are you not, Mr. Holmes?"

"Of course."

"Brilliant. Then you will be pleased to know that we also have excursions planned to the north, all the way up to Sapporo. You will have to take a ferry over to Hokkaido. It is a little risky, what with the Japanese and the Russian taking potshots at each others' boats, but I suppose that a detective is not going to be phased by a little spot of danger. Right, Mr. Holmes?"

"Right."

"And we must not neglect what we in the Legation call the regional cities. You know: Sendai, Nagoya, Osaka, Hiroshima, and even all the way to the south, to Nagasaki. I do hope you will not object if we leave off the island of Shikoku?"

"Not at all."

"Brilliant. There are just not enough people there, let alone those who are devoted to your adventures. Now. What is the next item on your schedule? The next item is your presence as the awarder of the prizes at the athletic events sponsored by our Legation and the twenty leading British firms that are doing business here in Japan. You really do not have to do anything except be there at the finish line and hand out the citation entitling the winners to their scholarships at Oxford. And why have we assigned you the task, Mr. Holmes? I am sure you are dying to know."

"Dying."

"Ah, yes. Quite the puzzle, isn't it? You see, all of the representatives of our British firms have been squabbling like schoolboys demanding that they should be the one to give the prize. So rather than choosing one of them and thereby creating a situation of one ingrate and nineteen malcontents, we came up with the brilliant idea of having you perform the task. All those chaps agreed that it was a top drawer decision as long as they had the opportunity to shake your hand and have you sign their latest copy of *The Strand*. You would be agreeable to doing that, would you not, Mr. Holmes?"

"Quite agreeable. How many events will be held?"

"Three. One each month beginning on the fifteenth of April, and then on the fifteenth of each succeeding month. And we are quite proud of the contests we have designed. Each will be progressively more difficult. The final one will be a bit grueling, and you will have to do a bit of climbing yourself, but I am sure you will not object, will you, Mr. Holmes?"

"Not in the least."

"Excellent. Excellent. Now then, I do believe that your brother, Sir Mycroft, has given you some preliminary data on a couple of sticky wickets we are facing here in Tokyo, has he not?"

"He has."

"Very well, then what are those situations? Strange secrets they are. I am sure you are eager to know more."

"I do believe that my heart is palpitating."

"Quite understandable. But do try to control yourself. We in His Majesty's Foreign Service have to face difficult situations like these all the time. Well, perhaps not like the most difficult one we are facing today, but I will get to that momentarily. First, we require your skills as a detective to try to find out what in the world happened to the poor American bloke they found floating in the Sumida River. Are you are aware of that situation, Mr. Holmes?"

"Somewhat. Wasn't that the case we solved this morning, Watson?"

I nodded, not sure whether to laugh or look bored.

"I beg your pardon, Mr. Holmes. You say you solved it?"

"Yes. Quite. Dr. Watson has a copy of the report in his pocket. We will leave it with you when we depart. And what is the second situation, please, Minister Humphrey?"

The fellow was temporarily at a loss for words since he was clearly not expecting the response he received. However, being the polished diplomat he was, he recovered quickly and moved on.

"The second sticky wicket, as I like to call them, is the disappearance of our Cultural Attaché Mr. Sean O'Neill, who took a properly scheduled and approved journey by ferry out to the island of Oshima, at the opening of Tokyo Bay. Are you familiar with that island, Mr. Holmes?"

"Not in the least."

"I feared as much. Very well, it is a volcanic island that is famed, and very proud of I might add, of its camellia blossoms. Not the cherry blossoms, which you have been enjoying since arriving in Tokyo, but the camellia blossoms, which appeared in late February. Quite the pleasant event. Entire trees, row upon row of them, covered with these lovely large blooms. Sean requested that he be permitted to attend their festival, and his request was approved. Now, you are asking, what happened to him?"

"The question was on the tip of my tongue."

"And so it should be. And the answer is that we do not know. No idea, whatsoever. Nothing. *Nada. Nichts. Absolument rien.* And therein, Mr. Sherlock Holmes, is your second assignment. Please, sir, find our boy. His disappearance is most embarrassing. Whitehall is very patient about these matters, but not for long."

"If you can furnish such data as you have, I shall give it my attention."

"Very well. I will have the latest dossier delivered to you. All I can say is that Sean arrived at the port of Atami. I assume you know all about that place."

"Not the foggiest."

"I feared as much. So how shall I put this without being indelicate? You should be aware that Atami is one of the great centers in Japan for tourists from all over the world. Now, do I have to spell out what that means, Mr. Holmes?"

"I can imagine."

"I am sure you can. Very well, now then, for the *pièce de résistance*: The wife of Mr. Grant Munro, our Envoy Extraordinary and Minister Plenipotentiary, the former Miss Ekaterina Federov. Had the lady married Mr. Grant immediately after he completed his degree at Cambridge, she would have learned by now how to behave as a proper diplomatic wife. But, sad to say, that did not happen. She was, quite frankly, well past her prime when she met him here in Tokyo less than a year ago. And since she was already established as a

47

nurse and a teacher, she had some fifteen years to become far too independent-minded and headstrong. Just what you might expect from an American. And she has this habit, as I believe Sir Mycroft has told you, of vanishing for several days at a time whenever she jolly well feels like it. And it just won't do. It won't do at all. It is terribly alarming to all of us."

"Is Mr. Munro not alarmed?"

"No. And that is the most annoying part of it all. He is positively smitten with her. Besotted, if you will. Bewitched, as far as I am concerned. He can hear no wrong said of her, or even the least hinted. He is all for progressive, egalitarian marriage. He is forever placing his arm around her shoulders, and he's all 'My darling; my dearest; my sweet one,' and those are just the terms he uses in public. What has been overheard of how he addresses his wife in private is not fit for repeating in polite company. Shocking. It makes the pages of *The Pearl* seem like *Mary Slessor's Diary*."

"Yes. That would be shocking were I familiar with either of those publications."

"No? Very well. It matters not. What matters is that he will not hear of anything said against her."

"Surely, Mr. Minister, you have had her followed. Where does she go?"

"Of course, we have had her followed. She takes herself down to Minato. First, she pays a visit to the Girls' School that is run by the Society of Friends out of Philadelphia, and then she stays in the house of a Japanese family that provides boarding for students."

"I fail to see the treachery in that. Please explain."

"Did your brother not fully pass on the data we had sent him? Oh well, it matters not. Here it is. This house in which she stays is just a few doors away from the house where a known Russian agent boards, and she makes regular visits to that house. His disguise, if I may call it that, is that he teaches mathematics at the Friends' School.

Not only that, but she sends him regular letters, all in code mind you. What is in those letters? I am sure you are desperate to know?"

"I am a desperate man, indeed."

"Right. We have been able to intercept all of them and copy them before they are passed on to the Czar's agent. How are we able to do that? We are able because we have recruited a young secretary in the school office, a simple young thing, hailing from Scranton, Pennsylvania, who is far from pretty and bordering on bovine. She is a faithful Quaker, but we assured her that she was helping us secure world peace. And, of course, we invite her to any of the parties we hold for our sailors when their ships are in port. As a result, she has been splendidly diligent. Never careless. Since the school serves *in loco parentis,* all correspondence to and from students and staff is opened and reviewed before being sent so as to avoid anything that should not be communicated. Our girl has the job of reviewing all correspondence, and so she copies everything that is received by the Russian agent. Quite the good little gem she is, Mr. Holmes. Do you see?"

"I do now. Thank you for enlightening me."

"Well now, the letters are in coded language, and we have not been able to completely decipher them, but what we have seen in them is very revealing, disturbing, and, if I may be so blunt, treacherous and treasonous."

"Ah, that is serious. But may I ask how you were able to discern treason in messages which you had not been able to decipher?"

"I only said, Mr. Holmes, that we were not able to *completely* decipher them. There was enough to convince us that the matter was extremely serious. Now, rather than going into it in detail, I will have copies of the messages delivered to you, and you can see for yourself. The immediate element that will strike you is that all of the salutations and closings are written in the Russian language, and are considered by those of us who are familiar with the Slavic languages, to be quite affectionate terms of endearment. Our good lady's relationship with this agent is highly suspect for quite unspeakable reasons and not merely matters of great import to the state."

"Oh, my. That is a concern."

"Yes, Mr. Holmes, it is indeed. You must know that the Russian Baltic fleet is due to arrive any day now in the waters of the East China Sea. Anything that would connect our Legation to the battle would be most unfortunate, as we are entirely neutral."

"Are we, indeed?" asked Holmes. "I thought we were rather better disposed to the Japanese?"

"If you must know, Mr. Holmes, our preferred result is that both sides would lose and that both their navies would be heavily damaged. That would leave our fleet paramount in the region, and both of them needing more vessels, which, of course, they would buy from us. Now do you understand, Mr. Holmes?"

"It is as clear as crystal. Thank you."

"Very well. That is really all I have to say to you this afternoon. Please do what you can as quickly as possible to find our missing attaché. And once you have done that, kindly furnish enough irrefutable evidence against Mrs. Munro, formerly Miss Federov, to send her packing, with or without her husband. Thank you, gentlemen. That will be all. Good day."

He strode over to the door and held it open for us. We rose and departed the room. Our diligent Tommy was waiting for us in the vestibule, sitting with his arms crossed over his chest. He jumped up from his chair on seeing us and bowed.

"Ah, Sherlock-san and Dr. John-san, I trust you had an excellent meeting with the Secretary. While I was waiting, I received some interesting news. May I share this news with you, gentlemen?"

"By all means," I said.

"Your first lecture has been confirmed. You have been given a very high honor. You will deliver your lecture in the *Kabuki-za*. Only the most respected of Japanese actors are ever allowed on stage at this place. It is a mark of the respect with which you are held in Japan, dear Sherlock-san."

"Please," said Holmes, "do thank whoever is to be thanked for the honor. I assume that those attending will be members of the Sherlock Holmes Society, those with nothing better to do than argue over the romanticized stories that our good doctor has written about me?"

"Oh, no, Sherlock-san. Those are the common people. They will not be allowed to attend until later. This lecture is reserved for the Prime Minister and his cabinet, and all of the diplomats from many countries, and the heads of the shrines and temples, and the leaders of our industries, and our most prestigious professors. It is a very noble crowd who will be listening to you."

"Oh, well, in that case, will I need a translator, or do they all speak English?"

"No, Sherlock-san. They all try to pretend that they speak English, but most do not beyond a few words. I have the great honor of serving as your translator. However, you may be sure, sir, that all of them have read your stories since they have all been translated into Japanese."

It dawned on me that I should have a word with my agent, Arthur Doyle, as I was not aware of having received any royalties for the sale of the stories in Japan. Pirated copies were to be expected in France, of course, but I had, perhaps naïvely, held the Japanese to a higher standard.

"Very well, then, Tommy," said Holmes. "We shall put on a capital show for all those dignitaries."

The lecture was to be given in two days, and I expected that Holmes would devote his time to polishing his delivery of his favorite speech, *The Science of Deduction,* and tailoring it specifically to the interests of the Japanese. I would recite one of my published stories as an introduction to the main event, but I could prepare for that while strolling through the streets of Tokyo, which I did. There was a broad boulevard that served as the perimeter of the Imperial Palace grounds, separated from the palace itself by a deep moat. The embankments were still gloriously adorned by cherry trees in bloom, and so I did the entire three-mile walk several times while rehearsing my delivery of the story. I invited Tommy to walk with me, but he declined, apparently more concerned about whatever Holmes might get himself up to than about me.

Around five o'clock on the day of the lecture, Tommy called for us and escorted us the several blocks through Ginza to the ornate white building where we would perform. The *Kabuki-za* was a most impressive building. The gleaming white exterior gave evidence of a mixing of Western architectural style with the traditional structures of Japan. The interior, however, rivaled any of the great opera houses of Europe, the Royal Opera House in Covent Garden, or even La Scala notwithstanding. In the spacious lobby all of the paintings, antiquities, and other *objets d'arte* that had been sent for the British cultural exchange were on display.

As expected, Holmes and I were led to the stage. A row of chairs stretched across the proscenium in front of the main curtain. We were seated, along with several others who I did not recognize, and I looked out in amazement at the full house in front of me. On the floor, to my right, were the *gaijin,* the foreigners, mostly British, who were dressed in formal finery as if attending the opening night of the opera. On my left were the leading members of the Japanese government and armed forces, some of whom were in formal Western dress, and others, the women especially, gloriously displaying every color of the rainbow in their stunning kimonos. The men's Japanese garb was subdued by comparison but elegant and impressive all the same.

A small lectern had been placed at the front of the stage, and I anticipated that Holmes and I would deliver our talks over the next ninety minutes and be on our way.

I had seriously underestimated the patience and endurance of a Japanese audience.

The evening was called to order by a chap that I assumed was the master of the theater. He spoke for some twenty minutes and was followed by the Minister of Culture, who did the same. Three more Japanese gentlemen, the Minister of Foreign Affairs, the Prime Minister himself and finally the representative of the Emperor.

Our very faithful helper, Tommy, was in a chair behind Holmes and me and was leaning forward so as to offer commentary and translation. The western diplomats and commercial barons were visibly restless, but the Japanese endured every repetitive speech, listening attentively and applauding warmly. It occurred to me that had this event been held in Royal Albert Hall, the audience by now would be snoring or finding excuses to walk out. Of course, had it been held in Carnegie Hall, the volatile New Yorkers would have heckled the speakers off the stage and chased them down Seventh Avenue.

Finally, it was the turn of the Envoy of Great Britain, Mr. Grant Munro, to speak. Wisely, he kept his remarks brief and witty. I confess that I was more interested in watching his wife, the object of our suspicions, as she sat in the front row of the foreigners, to see how she responded to her husband's public persona. I had to give her credit – she did not betray an iota of disrespect for the man and the office she was betraying to a rival foreign power. Instead, she was all rapt attention, never looking anything but adoring of the handsome, articulate man behind the podium. She was a consummate actress and earned my respect.

When it came my turn, I strode to the podium, accompanied by Tommy as my translator, and recited one of the most popular of the stories I had written about Sherlock Holmes – *The Adventure of the Speckled Band.* I had been advised that the Japanese, although outwardly not particularly religious, had an abiding fascination with all things evil and macabre, and, of course, anything that was tied to murderous doctors and poisonous snakes from India stirred their blood. I was quite sure that everyone in the hall knew how the story would end, but they hung on to my every word. I could hear many grown women whimpering like frightened children as I described the horrific way that the villain had planned to murder poor Miss Helen Stoner. They all applauded generously when I came to the end. Dr. Grimesby Roylott was sitting dead and gruesome in his chair, and they seemed quite convinced that justice had been done.

Holmes then ascended to the podium, accompanied by loud but orderly applause, and delivered his most famous lecture, *The Science of Deduction*. Readers of my stories are aware that, from time to time, Holmes has accused me of romanticizing and sensationalizing his adventures for the sake of entertaining my readers. But on this particular evening, our roles were reversed. Holmes clearly enjoyed adding to the horrific and gory details of the crimes, dwelling on the depths of depravity, and expanding on the scandalous behavior of the criminal minds of England. The verbal outbursts from the men and, again, the childish whimpering from the women, was sufficient evidence required to indicate that a good time was being had by all.

A brief reception was held for us following the event. For the first half-hour, both Holmes and I were monopolized by various Japanese dignitaries who graciously bowed and gave generous compliments, but who, if I were to allow myself uncharitable thoughts, might also be seizing the opportunity both to practice their English and, feigning modesty, demonstrate their masterful knowledge of detective stories. All the while, I could see Mr. and Mrs. Munro patiently waiting until our hosts were done with us before approaching to chat. When the opportunity to do so finally came, they walked to our side and shook our hands. For several minutes, we exchanged chit chat about the similarities of the weather in Tokyo and London, both being damp with London being colder, and then we moved on to a review of our tour of the country. The two of them made a most elegant and charming couple, smiling warmly and making no end of witty remarks that brought an involuntary smile even to the face of the taciturn Sherlock Holmes.

Yet again, there was not a single hint of duplicity in the performance given by Mrs. Effie Munro. Not once did I catch her averting her gaze to see what else was going on in the room or see her paying less than complete attention to the conversation taking place amongst us. A very polished performer indeed, I had to admit.

Chapter Seven   Our New Friends

Our Envoy confirmed that Sherlock Holmes would be the honored guest who would award the prize at the upcoming footrace, sponsored by the British Legation and Industries. It would take place in just a few days and would involve three complete circuits around the Imperial Palace grounds. The men would run their race first, followed by the women. I was surprised to hear that Japanese women were permitted to engage in such a contest.

I asked, "Is His Majesty's Government encouraging the emancipation of women and female suffrage here in Japan?"

"Oh, good heavens, no, Dr. Watson," replied Mr. Munro. "The British Empire does not interfere in the cultural practices of foreign countries, not even in our own colonies. But the current regime in Japan has been on a tear towards becoming a modern industrial nation. They have a desperate need for dedicated, reliable laborers in all their new factories, so they have to reverse centuries of demanding that young women remain in the fathers' homes in their villages. Now they must become independent, move to the cities, and work in the factories. The request for us to have a women's athletic event, as well as a men's, came from the Diet. So, of course, we went along. And it should be a splendid spectacle, don't you agree?"

I nodded my agreement but was not entirely convinced. We continued the conversation for a few more minutes and then made to take our leave. To my surprise, Mrs. Munro caught Sherlock Holmes off-guard with her final question.

"Mr. Holmes," she said in a manner that bordered on flirtatious, "is it really true that in your entire career you have been bested by only *one* woman? Tell the truth now, was Irene Adler the only woman to have proven to be smarter than the country's finest detective?" She then laughed infectiously.

Holmes appeared to be momentarily at a loss for words, but recovered and replied, somewhat imperiously, "I assure you, Madam, that there has indeed been only one woman who can claim that distinct accomplishment."

"Only one *so far,*" she responded, again followed by a pleasant laugh.

Yet again, I was struck by the brazen ability of this American woman. I was quite certain that, given her access to secretive sources of information, she must have known or at least suspected that Sherlock Holmes had been sent by Whitehall to do more than entertain the Japanese populace. But here she was joyfully taunting him. It would not surprise me at all if she joined the select rank now inhabited only by Irene Adler.

Sherlock Holmes prides himself on eschewing emotions and depending on cool reason alone when involved in a serious case. That sense of pride, however, has been known to invade his emotional state in spite of his determination not to allow it. As we walked back to the hotel, I noticed that Holmes had quickened his pace, a sure sign that his anger had been piqued by the fearless taunting of Mrs. Munro. Upon reaching the hotel, he immediately retired to his room, without our customary few moments of tobacco and brandy, and without so much as a pleasant 'Good night, Watson.'

When I descended the stairs to the breakfast room, the next morning, I found Holmes already into his notes and files, his rice porridge and nearly raw morsels of fish already devoured. Without so much as a pleasant 'Good morning, Watson,' he immediately launched into our schedule for the day.

"I have sent notice to the Second Minister, that Humphrey chap, as well as to Tommy, that I wish to advance a portion of our schedule."

"I am not surprised, Holmes. So, do tell, where are we going today?"

"To the School for Girls run by the Society of Friends. It is the place where the fellow that Humphrey identified as the Russian agent is working, using his role as a teacher of mathematics to cover his treachery. It is also the place to which Mrs. Munro's notes and letters are sent on a regular basis."

"Ah yes, the ones that are partially in code and replete with affectionate greetings and closings in Russian."

"Precisely. The good Quakers who are in charge of the place had requested that we come and speak and assured us that they could accommodate a last-minute change in schedule, since all they have to do is haul the girls out of their classes and into the Assembly Hall. Blessedly, we shall not have to endure two hours of Japanese formalities. I intend to take the measure of the Russian and attempt to deduce just what he and our dear Mrs. Effie are up to. I assured them that you would be prepared to recite an appropriate story, and I will again give them my lecture."

"I shall be so prepared, although I take it that both of us will have to Bowdlerize our remarks somewhat, given the religious and irenic sensibilities of the good Quakers."

"Precisely. It would never do to provoke the heating of the blood of the peaceful folk nor create palpitations in the hearts of their young charges."

A group of Quakers from Philadelphia had, in 1887, established a school for girls in a pleasant suburban area of Tokyo, the Minato-ku, about three miles south of the hotel and Palace grounds. Tommy advised us that it would take us at least an hour to walk the distance, and so he quickly arranged a taxi.

The Friends School, or *Fuendo Gakuen,* was housed in an impressive set of wooden buildings, all whitewashed and immaculate. I was surprised by the large number of Japanese girls, several hundred of them ranging in age from ten through seventeen, who were all attired in starched and pressed uniforms. I had not thought that the upper classes of Japanese families would want their children exposed to daily doses of a distinctly American version of the Christian religion, but the emphasis on academic achievement and the opportunity to learn English had obviously trumped any concerns of religious indoctrination.

After a brief meeting with Headmistress Esther Biddle, we were led into the Assembly Hall, where the entire student body had gathered. They stood up as we entered, and more or less in unison bowed to us. In a manner similar to the previous evening, first I and then Holmes spoke to them. I recited the story I usually did when addressing young people, *The Man with the Twisted Lip.* It was ideal for such a gathering as it created all sorts of fears of murder and terror but ended happily with a touch of romance. Tommy did, as always, a superb job of translating it, and the girls sat spellbound. Several of the younger ones in the front rows grabbed the hand of the one sitting next to them and acted as if they were thoroughly frightened. The tune of *Three Little Maids from School* floated through my mind.

I knew that while I was speaking, Holmes would be intensely surveying the audience, attempting to identify the Slav math teacher. As I concluded my recitation, I turned and passed Holmes as he took his place at the lectern. He indicated with his eyes and chin, the direction in which I should look. Upon sitting down, I looked out to the hall and quickly identified our suspect. There were only a handful of male teachers in the crowd and, since almost all of the students were of short stature, except for a few of the seniors, they were easy to spot. They all looked like earnest American lads from Philadelphia, but there was one fellow, seated near the back who appeared to be a recent refugee from Siberia. He was tall, fair-skinned, and distinctly square-headed. I assumed that Holmes had already devised a means of speaking to him following our presentation.

And so he did. As soon as the lecture was finished and the girls had applauded long and enthusiastically and bowed many more times, Holmes accosted the headmistress and earnestly sought her assistance.

"Miss Biddle, you are most welcome," Holmes replied to her effusive words of thanks. "Might I ask for your assistance in a small matter that I need to resolve immediately?"

"Why, of course, Mr. Holmes," the good lady answered. "I cannot imagine what our school might do to assist a famous detective, but we shall be honored to help in whatever way we can."

"Ah, you are most kind, Headmistress. You see, in a few days, I am scheduled to give a lecture to the Japanese Society of Mathematicians, and I confess, I do not know a co-sign from a derivative, and I am frightfully afraid of looking like a fool in front of such an august gathering. Would it be possible to seek the confidential advice of your math teacher? Could she be spared for a few minutes from her duties?"

"Why, of course, Mr. Holmes, we can look after you and happy to do so, except that our math teacher is not a 'she' but a 'he.' Mr. Lobachevesky is a highly renowned mathematician who, for unfortunate political reasons, is in exile from his own country. But we are most fortunate to have him as a member of our faculty. And I must say, the senior girls and some of my young lady teachers are quite smitten with him," she said, smiling.

We were led into the austere teachers' workroom and waited at a plain table until the door opened, and a tall young Slav entered. He was smiling broadly and eagerly approached Sherlock Holmes. I feared for a moment that he might engulf my friend in the infamous

Russian bear hug, but he refrained and extended a large hand at the end of a long arm.

"Gospadin Holmes," he said pleasantly. "I am Nicolai Ivanovich Lobachevesky. It is to me honor very great to meet you. If help I can be to you, it for me is very good, yah."

He sat at the table, stretched his long legs under it, and sloped at a forty-degree angle to the floor.

"So good of you to come to our assistance," said Holmes. "We shan't take up too much of your time. If your students are anything like our British schoolboys, they should not be left on their own for more than five minutes, or all sorts of mischief will ensue."

The math teacher let out a loud belly laugh. "Gospadin Holmes. Japanese girl student could not be more unlike English schoolboy. Girls here, very smart. But are excellent sheep. Cannot imagine they do not behave. Not is problem."

"Are you telling me," asked Holmes, his eyebrows rising, "that a Russian novelist would have nothing to write about in Japan?"

Another belly laugh burst out. "Ah, Gospadin Holmes, you know well Russian writers. If they cannot find crime and punishment or war and peace, what is to write about? Behavior of good Japanese students does not work for Russian writer." He laughed again.

"Very well then, sir. Permit me then, without fear of a student uprising, to seek your advice. It is a small thing, but I need to come up with the name of a valuable mathematical treatise to use as an example of something that might be stolen or become a cause of a crime amongst mathematicians. As I have only a very weak knowledge of your field of expertise, and I dread the thought of appearing like a fool, especially since I am representing His Majesty's Government, could I ask you to help me? Is there a famous work of mathematics that I could use as such an example?"

Mr. Lobachevsky nodded immediately. "I give you name of very famous recent publication that not only is famous but also has been stolen. Very big story in world of mathematicians. Called it is *Analytic and algebraic topology of locally Euclidean metrization of infinitely differentiable Riemannian manifold.* Japanese professors all know this paper."

"Wonderful. And from whom was it stolen?"

The teacher raised his head and spoke to the top of the far wall. "Written it is by Nicolai Ivanovich Lobachevesky. That is I. Stolen from me it is by the agents of the Devil, the Great Oppressor of the People, Czar Nicholas. It is very great crime. All mathematicians are knowing about it, and if they know not, they must be made knowing about it. This is good example for you, yah?"

"Ah, excellent. Watson, did you get the name of that treatise? You have it? Yes. Splendid."

Here Holmes paused and looked quizzically at the Slav. "Forgive me, Doctor Lobachevesky," he said, "But as you know, I am a detective, and I cannot resist being curious when some data come my way that is unexpected. Would you mind terribly if I asked you about your history? You have said some things, enough to whet my appetite. I perceive that there is a story behind the presence of a famous Russian mathematician who is no longer teaching in an academy in Moscow or St. Petersburg, but is found in a school for Japanese girls. How, doctor, did this come about? I do hope you don't mind my asking."

"Not sir, at all. I honored by your interest."

He again looked up at the wall, folded his long arms across his chest, and took in a slow breath. "I am never forget that day, it is three years ago. I am teaching in the University of Vladivostok. I am only lecturer but on my way to be great professor of mathematics at best university, like you say, in Moscow or St. Petersburg. I am just publish my paper, my treatise on which I am working very hard for three years. But we have at university a *soviet*, how you say, a small committee that is struggling to bring freedom to proletariat, to all Russian people. I am member of this committee. We are making peaceful requests of change in university, in local government. We do not want revolution, only we want reform, like they have in Germany or your England. We hold public meeting and tell working people about need to unite and bring change. That night, at midnight I hear knock on my door. I have friend in police force, and he is at my door. He say me that I must run away or agents of the Czar will kill me or send me to *gulag*. They are waiting for me in morning to come to university. I say him no, is not possible. But I see he is serious and afraid for me. He say me that boat is leaving in three hours from Vladivostok port to go to Japan, and I must get on. I say I do this, and maybe I return if problem goes away. Problem does not go away. I arrive Otaru, and I wait, and I hear that other members of soviet are made to disappear. Letters come from friends and tell me do not come back. Not safe. My treatise is stolen and plagiarized by old professor in Moscow who is friend to third cousin of Czar. I have nothing. On streets of Sapporo, I meet American missionaries who are good to me and give me food and clothes and I say them my story. They say me come to Tokyo, and they find job for me in American Christian school. I come here. They welcome me and I teach mathematics to girls. It is very humble, but I am grateful. My career as professor is over until, maybe, there is revolution in my country and I can return. For now, I am happy here. Students like me. Teachers like me. I teach very simple things. In Russia, I am good athlete, and so they give me post of athletic coach to senior girls. It does not need brain, but I am safe. That is my story, Gospadin Holmes."

He smiled and shrugged his wide shoulders.

Holmes returned the smile and rose from his chair. "I regret, doctor, that I am only a humble detective and cannot bring about the great changes your country is crying out for. But I assure you that my hopes are with you, and I look forward to the day when you can return to your calling."

"You are good to me, *spacibo moi drug*. It, as you say, is honor to me, to help you and have you listen to story." He stood as well, and this time did not refrain from placing Sherlock Holmes in an enormous bear hug that was held for several seconds longer than I knew Holmes could tolerate. Then the fellow left the room, smiling and thanking us several more times before closing the door behind him.

Holmes sat down again, and instinctively reached for his cigarette case. I quickly reached out and put my hand on his arm.

"Holmes, you cannot smoke in here. The Quakers would shoot you."

He scowled and put the case back in his pocket. "Very well then, Watson, we shall contemplate without the aid of tobacco. So, tell me. What did you conclude concerning our teacher?"

"A rather tragic story, I must say."

"Good heavens, Watson. You cannot be seriously saying that you believed him?"

I was quite taken aback, since I, in fact, had believed him. "Apparently, Holmes, you did not."

"Elementary, Watson. It is not without cause that there is a common riddle concerning Russians that is known throughout Europe."

"I'm afraid I am not familiar with it."

"It goes, 'How can you tell when a Russian is lying?' Can you guess the answer?"

"No, I fear I cannot."

"His lips move." Holmes followed these words with a thin, smug smile. "Really, Watson, can you not see that the course of events described has been just a bit too convenient and coincidental to be believed? Please observe what we were told: A young professor of mathematics, which is a highly desirable trait as perceived by the Japanese, desperate as they are to become a modern, industrial world power, just happens to arrive in Japan immediately prior to the outbreak of hostilities between Japan and Russia. He coincidentally meets up with sympathetic Americans shortly after fleeing from the nearest major Russian city, and they recommend that he take a post at a school in Tokyo which just happens to have an appropriate opening, just happens to be American and protected from Japanese aggression, just happens to be associated with the new wife of the British Envoy, who just happens to have immediate family and, no doubt, current relatives who just happen to be from Vladivostok. It beggars belief that such coincidences could all be the result of mere chance."

"Hmmm. I suppose you have a point there, Holmes. But I still think the chap came across as rather guileless."

"No, Watson, he came across as a master of guile. And I am quite certain that if we are able to review and decode the messages sent to him from Mrs. Munro, we shall be able to break their conspiracy wide open."

Chapter Eight The Green Ribbon

During the next few days, we delivered several more lectures, including one, hastily arranged, to the Japanese mathematicians. They gave due respect to a famous foreigner but were otherwise not particularly enthusiastic. When Holmes made reference to the stolen treatise by our Russian, he drew completely blank stares and quickly switched his example of a nefarious theft to one in which a professor purloined a bottle of vintage sake from the desk of a colleague. This brought forth nods of recognition.

The weekend brought the first of the three British-sponsored athletic events. The lofty goals were clear: First, promote Japanese interest in the approaching 1908 Olympics; second, recruit brilliant young runners to attend Oxford and then have them represent our Empire; third, inspire sufficient independence in young Japanese women to have them leave the farms and join the factories.

The twelve-mile run—three times around the grounds of the Imperial Palace—would be demanding but only because of the distance. The course itself was entirely flat. The prizes, a ceremonial green ribbon and medallion, a select green kimono, a scholarship to Oxford, and all due fame and renown, had served to attract a large crowd of runners. Entry was open to all comers for this first race. The second and third races, however, would only be open to those who had qualified in the preceding races. It brought patriotic joy to my English heart to see the streets lined with watchers, waving small Union Jacks held in the same hand as the flag of the rising sun.

It appeared to me that well over a thousand young men had gathered for their race, and perhaps as many as five hundred women. As with all things we had observed so far in Japan, women were honored and respected, but men were favored and took precedence. And so the men's race began in the cool of the early morning, followed by the women's at ten o'clock. Holmes and I were present at the finish line and watched the runners stagger towards it. Before the top three could be presented to the visiting dignitaries, their coaches helped them don a kimono, as it would not have been seemly to have them appear in front of us, especially with photographers present, in their athletic attire. Several officials from our Legation were present, as well as the top brass of our overseas industries. I was somewhat surprised that our Envoy and his striking American wife were not on hand for the winners of the men's race, but showed up in time for the women's.

"As I said, Doctor Watson," said Mr. Munro, "we are doing our part to enhance the independent role of young women. The would-be shoguns and daimyos in the Diet are counting on us."

The three winners of the women's race were all mere wisps of girls, none more than ninety pounds. The top two hundred finishers were recorded, as they were then permitted to participate in the second race. There were a few taller girls in the lot, but, again, the great majority of them were tiny things that a strong wind would blow away. Mrs. Munro took the time to congratulate every one of those who completed the race, regardless of how long it took them. Her warm praise appeared to me to be utterly sincere.

"Now gentlemen," said Mr. Munro, placing his hands on the shoulders of both Holmes and me. "I believe that a pleasant lunch, courtesy of His Majesty, would be in order. What say, men? The

Rokumeikan puts on an excellent spread, and it is just a few blocks from here. Will you be my guests?"

He asked most graciously, but, of course, it was not an invitation we could refuse.

"The Olympics," began the Envoy over the first course, "will be held in Rome in three years from now and a great deal of national pride is at stake. The last round, hosted by the Americans in St. Louis, was a fiasco, and all of Europe is determined to make a better go of it this time. The Japanese are determined to show that they can compete on the world's stage and, given the present state of war with Russia, show that they can stand up on the track as well as on the battlefield. Over the next three years, they will select the men who will be c*itius , altius, fortius* to represent the land of Nippon."

"And the women, Jack," added his wife in a friendly rebuke.

"Of course, darling, the women as well. There will be several more events for them this time around."

"And someday," she added, "they will have the same number of events open to them as the men. Isn't that right, Jack?"

"Yes, yes, darling. Entirely correct, darling. Entirely correct."

As I sportsman, I had a genuine interest in the topic. Holmes was not and had none. He feigned interest, however, as he had noticed our Russian agent in the crowd of male participants.

"I could not help but notice," he said, "that one of the teachers from the Quakers' school we visited a few days ago was in the race. I had not thought of that sect as being particularly competitive in athletics."

I noticed an involuntary reaction from Mrs. Munro, and I was quite certain that Holmes had seen it as well.

Without missing a beat, she coolly replied, "As a matter of fact, Mr. Holmes, there were three teachers and ten students from *Furendo Gakuen*. Which of them did you recognize?"

"Ah, the math teacher. Yes, I believe it was math that he said he taught."

"Oh, you must mean Nick. I hear you had a chat with him after your lecture. He is not a bad runner himself, and he coaches the girls' team. They let him know that if they had to run in the British races, so did he. He's a good sport, and so he jolly well ran the race. Some of his girls came in early enough to qualify for the next round, and Nick just made it in himself. Knowing him, he probably had to stop at least ten times for a cigarette. If he shows up for classes next week, I will be surprised."

She added yet another of her infectious little laughs when she finished. I could see that Holmes was more than a little nonplussed by this woman's triumphal confidence.

"Ah, yes, madam. That was the chap. You appear to be quite familiar with the school."

"My wife," interjected Mr. Munro, "is a member of their advisory board and keeps close track of what all is going on over there." He was quite beaming with pride as he spoke.

"Ah, are you?" replied Holmes. "I did not know that you were a member of that sect."

Here she laughed again and smiled back at Holmes. "Oh, really, Mr. Holmes. I'm sure you know perfectly well that I am anything but a peace-loving Quaker. I'm a Baptist, and in America, we are far removed from the Society of Friends. We pray regularly for their enlightenment and salvation. But over here, scarcity of all brands of Protestants compels us to get along."

Again she smiled, even though she had caught Holmes out on his feigning of ignorance. I was starting to quite enjoy the emerging battle of wits that was happening in front of me. So far, the lady was winning.

"I have no doubt you are quite right, madam," said Holmes. He then wisely changed the subject and moved back to idle chat about our lecture tour and the next two races.

"Yes, right," began the Envoy. "The next race will be held in four weeks, on the fifteenth of May. It will be shorter than this one, but much more demanding. By Jove, it will separate the men from the boys."

"And the women from the girls, Jack."

"Yes, yes. Of course, darling. And the women from the girls. Are you familiar, Mr. Holmes, with the small mountains they call Takeo and Jinba?"

"No, Excellency, I cannot say that I am."

"Right. Well, sir, you are going to be, since you will have to be present at the top of Jinba to award the prizes, and I am afraid that the only way to get there is to hike. The runners have to run up the trail to the top of Takeo and then through the forest until they reach the summit of Jinba. How far is it, darling? What would you say?"

Mrs. Munro replied, "At least ten miles, Jack. And it's up and down the whole way. But don't worry, Mr. Holmes, you can take the shortcut directly to the top of Jinba. It's a bit demanding, but the forest is pleasant, and the views are out of this world."

Yet again, she looked Holmes in the eye and smiled at him.

"I shall look forward to it, madam," he replied and smiled back. "Permit me to ask, if you will, what then is the final race? If a ten-mile course across mountain tops is only the penultimate, what could possibly be more demanding?"

Mr. Munro did not immediately answer. He then lowered his head and spoke in a quiet voice. "I fear, sir, that I am not at liberty yet to disclose that. It is still being negotiated. Some diplomatic issues, you know."

"Oh Jack," chimed in Mrs. Munro. "This is Sherlock Holmes you're talking to; the world's most famous detective. He must know more secrets than anyone else in your Empire. You can tell him."

"More secrets," Munro replied, "than anyone, my dear? With the exception of his older brother, I would think. Right, Mr. Holmes?

Yes, right, well then, I shall tell you. The final race is to the top of the highest mountain in the nation."

"You mean," I blurted, "they have to *run* to the top of Mount Fuji?"

"Precisely, doctor. That is what I mean. Now there's a challenge and a half, don't you think?"

I said nothing and just nodded, the thought dawning on me that we might have to climb Fuji as well if we were to be there to award the prizes. Holmes's thinking took a different tack.

"You must forgive me, Excellency, but what could be the diplomatic issues connected with such a race? I am aware that the mountain is sacred to the people of Japan, but hundreds of visiting foreigners climb it every summer, do they not?"

"Right, Mr. Holmes. Right. But they do not encounter the Emperor of Japan waiting at the summit to congratulate them."

I let out a low whistle of awe. "I must say, that would be a diplomatic coup. Might you truly be able to pull that one off, Mr. Munro?"

"If we do, it will not depend on anything we do. I assume that you have heard that the Russian fleet has been spotted in the East China Sea?"

"I was aware of that," said Holmes. This was surprising, since it was news to me.

"The Prime Minister," whispered the Envoy, "has called up every ship in the Japanese Navy. Within a few days, there will be a battle royal somewhere on the high seas. If Russia is victorious, the Emperor will not likely be seen in public for a decade. If Japan wins, which our intelligence now tells us is a possibility, then his presence at our event will be quite the opportunity for the country to strut its place on the world's stage. Our position, of course, is entirely neutral, and I will have to leave it to your imagination as to who we are favoring."

"Favoring is one thing," said Holmes. "But who are you betting on?"

"Ah ha, Mr. Holmes, now that is pushing me too far. Terribly sorry, old chap, but I'll have to order you another gin and tonic and let your famous mind think on that one." He slapped his hand down on the table, let out a brief laugh, and called the waiter.

As we stood and prepared to part, Mr. Munro approached us and placed his hand on Holmes's shoulder.

"I noticed on your itinerary that you will be spending a few days down around Hakone and Atami. While you are there, you really must try the hot springs and the *onsen*. Really, quite relaxing. And if, by chance, you hear anything about a British cultural attaché, do let me know. I appear to have lost one. He was last seen some two months ago on his way to the camellia flower festival on Oshima Island and has not been seen or heard from since. His name is Sean O'Neill, lovely chap. All friendly and outgoing, but not exactly the brightest star in the sky. Typically Irish, you know. Thanks awfully, gentlemen."

Chapter Nine   Russian to a Conclusion

ur travels to various places in the country began the following week. A full day on the train took us to Sendai, a large regional city on the east coast about two hundred miles north of Tokyo. It prided itself on its university but otherwise was primarily a fishing center. Holmes delivered his lecture, translated as always by Tommy, in one of the large lecture halls at the Tohoku College. To my surprise, there were women students as well as men present. Finding such enlightened liberal practices this far away from the nation's capital was quite commendable.

The city also had a long and pleasant beach from whence the fishing boats depart every morning, dark and early, and return at the end of the day bearing their catch. The prevailing winds from the west render the sea usually calm and tranquil. Indeed, as Holmes and I stood on the sand and looked out over the endless, blue, peaceful Pacific, I contemplated how this place must have brought serenity to the soul for centuries and would, I was sure, do so for centuries to come.

The calendar read the twenty-ninth of May, and the warm summer season had begun. A soft breeze blew I from the sea, enhancing my sense of tranquility. My pleasant contemplations were not to last and were loudly interrupted by Tommy's shouting. I turned to see him running up the beach toward us, waving a piece of paper in his hand.

"Sherlock-san! Dr. John-san!" he was screaming. "Please! Look! Very important!"

He kept sprinting until he reached, and then, all out of breath, he thrust the telegram into Holmes's hand. Holmes read it quickly and then handed it to me.

"A nice little note from Mycroft," he said.

It ran:

SHERLOCK: JAPANESE AND RUSSIAN NAVIES BATTLED YESTERDAY AT TSUSHIMA. RUSSIAN FLEET DESTROYED. JAPAN VICTORIOUS WITH FEW LOSSES. IMPORTANCE OF EVENT CANNOT BE OVERSTATED. NOW CRITICAL THAT ALL PARTIES RELATED TO HIS MAJESTY'S GOVERNMENT APPEAR COMPLETELY NEUTRAL, INCLUDING OUR SUSPECT. I CANNOT MOVE ON SUSPECT WITHOUT PROOF. GET IT FOR ME, AND NOT YOUR MERE CONJECTURE. M. H.

I looked at Holmes in disbelief. "This is amazing, Holmes. The Czar sent his entire Baltic Fleet to re-capture Port Arthur. It is an enormous loss for the Russians."

"And a monumental victory for the Japanese, a veritable sea change," he replied. He then took me by the arm and led me out of earshot of Tommy.

"Watson, if it is found out that our charming missionary is a Russian agent, then all hell will break loose, and Japan might very well declare Great Britain a hostile nation. We need to find out just what she has been doing and do so rather quickly."

I nodded my agreement, and we moved off the lovely sand and back into the city.

Two days later, we met again with Redvers Humphrey in his Legation office. The news of the incredible victory was all over the newspapers. Posters were plastered onto every available piece of wall, and the flag of Japan had been raised and attached to every possible pole. The people of Tokyo, who are normally inscrutable in their passivity, were beaming with smiles. The portable shrines, whose removal from the temples happened only on sacred occasions, were being carried through the streets, followed by jubilant crowds, all dressed in traditional celebratory garb and banging and blowing on anything that would make a noise.

"You are wanting to know," he said, "how this event will affect your obligations. Am I correct?"

"Most certainly," said Holmes.

"Really not much at all. It is going to have a much more significant effect on all of us who will remain here after you are gone. You are wondering why I say that?"

"In wonder and amazement."

"Ah, I thought you would be. We have just had word from Whitehall that His Majesty is now prepared to recognize Japan as a major world power. You do know what that means for our Legation, I assume."

"I fear I do not, Minister."

"No? Pity. It means that our Legation will disappear and be no more."

That sounded absurd, and I interjected and said as much.

"Oh no, Dr. Watson, it is entirely reasonable. You see our humble office will have the title of Legation removed and will soon be elevated to a full-fledged *Embassy*. Our Envoy will soon be promoted to an Ambassador. Now, I am sure you are about to ask me what the Americans are going to do. Am I correct, Mr. Holmes?"

"You took the words right out of my mouth, Minister."

"The Americans are going to follow our example and do the same thing. They will also recognize Japan as the power it is, on the same level as they do France, or Italy, or even the Court of St. James.

You will agree that this is a highly significant turn of events in global diplomacy, will you not, Mr. Holmes?"

"Yes, Minister; in total agreement."

"Now then, shall we deal with the more … ah … sensitive matters at hand?"

"I recall that those matters were the purpose of our meeting you."

"Quite so. Now then, since we last met, I have intercepted several more messages sent by a certain lady to a certain arithmetic teacher and had the phrases written in Russian all translated. Would you wish to see them, Mr. Holmes?"

"Yes, Minister. I would so wish."

He motioned to us to have a seat in front of his desk. He strutted to the other side, sat down, and handed a file to Holmes. I watched as Holmes opened it. The contents consisted of about twenty items, all made up of two pages of papers and pinned together.

"The top page, gentlemen," Humphrey said, "is the copy our helpful Quaker lady made of the messages sent by Mrs. Federov-Munro. The attached page contains the translations from the Russian that she used in the salutations and closings. I believe that you will find them very revealing."

The one on the top was the most recent. It read:

Милая моя:

> How brilliant of you to hold back from winning the race. It is an excellent strategy to let the others underestimate you. But now you move on to the next level. I will be there again to cheer you on.
>
> Ты чудесная.   Your Effie.

The page underneath it explained:

Милая моя in our script reads: milaya moya. It means "My Sweet."

The second one hit closer to home and read:

Любимая моя:

Did you enjoy the talks given by Sherlock Holmes and Dr. Watson at your school? I have listened to them as well. They are quite entertaining, even for Englishmen. I was imagining you, Солнышко моё, as you listened to them.

Ты чудесная, Your Effie.

The third one was particularly alarming and read:

Ангел мой,

The first battle will soon be upon us. You must do everything we have practiced and what your leader has told you. If you do, we will be victorious. Ты такая добрая, but you must also be determined. We are one with each other.

Люблю тебя всем сердцем, всей душою,

Your Effie

The other notes were all of the same order. In my notebook, I copied down the various phrases used in the Cyrillic script, the words as they would appear in Latin script, and the translations provided. They were all very personal and affectionate, distressingly so.

Зайчик моя - *zaichik moya* - My bunny:

Радость моя - *radost moya* - My joy

Солнышко моё - *solnyshka moyo* - My sunshine

Милая моя - *milaya moya* - My sweet

Любимая моя - *lyubimaya moya* - My sweetheart

Дорогая моя - dorogaya moya - My dear

Ангел мой - *angel moy* - My angel

Ты такая красивая - *ti takaya krasivaya* - You are [so] beautiful

Ты красивая - *ti krasivaya* - You are lovely

Ты чудесная - *ti chudesnaya* - You are wonderful

Ты милая -*ti milaya* - You are sweet

Ты нежная - *ti nezhnaya* - You are gentle

Ты такая добрая - *ti takaya dobraya* - You are kind

Я тебя люблю - *ya tebya lyublyu* - I love you

Люблю тебя всем сердцем, всей душою - *lyublyu tebya vsem
  sertsem, vsey dushoyu* – I love you with all my heart,
  with all my soul

Любовь моя, приди ко мне - *lyubov moya, pridi ka mne* - Come
to me, my love

Моё сердце полно любви - *moyo sertse polno lyubvi* - My
heart is full of love

Я буду всегда любить тебя - *ya budu vsegda lyubit tebya* - I will
always love you

"Do you see what I mean, gentlemen? The contents may be coded, but the illicit connection between the lady and the teacher is rather blatant, is it not?"

I agreed. "It is, rather."

Holmes merely nodded and said nothing.

"Now, gentlemen, I have saved the most incriminating until the last. Read this."

He thrust a final note that he had been withholding from us into Holmes's chest.

It read:

Ангел мой:

The news of the battle and the loss to Russia has made our presence in Japan very dangerous. I am working on a plan to have us escape and live in England. You, like the child of the moon that you are, must leave your family of bamboo cutters and return to your new home beyond the summit of Fuji. But it must wait until your final great victory at the summit, in which you will trounce all your opponents.

Я буду всегда любить тебя,

Your Effie.

Holmes's face was impassive, as it often becomes when matters of great pitch and moment are presented to him. He merely nodded to the Minister and said, "I assume that we may keep these copies?"

"You may, Mr. Holmes, and I am sure that you will now ask if you have the entire file."

"I assumed that I had."

"Ah, well, you assumed wrongly. There is one more that remains a mystery. It was written almost entirely in code, and we have not yet been able to crack it. But we shall, by George, we shall."

He handed a final page to us. It ran as follows:

My diligent one:

The problem you must solve may be expressed as:

$6x^2 + 11x - 35 = 0$

To the best of my memory, the solution is:

$$x = \frac{-(11) \pm \sqrt{(11)^2 - 4(6)(-35)}}{2(6)}$$

$$= \frac{-11 \pm \sqrt{121 + 840}}{12}$$

$$= \frac{-11 \pm \sqrt{961}}{12} = \frac{-11 \pm 31}{12}$$

$$= \frac{-11 - 31}{12}, \frac{-11 + 31}{12}$$

$$= -\frac{42}{12}, \frac{20}{12} = -\frac{7}{2}, \frac{5}{3}$$

The solution is $x = {}^{-7}/_2, {}^5/_3$

I hope this is helpful to you.

I do love you, my brilliant one,

Your Effie.

Both Holmes and I stared at it. I could not resist making the obvious observation.

"It's all Greek to me."

Holmes gave me a sideways look. "Oh, please, Watson, please."

But then he smiled. "To me, as well. But I assume that the Minister's codebreakers will solve it forthwith. Am I correct in assuming that, Minister?"

"Quite so. Quite so indeed, Mr. Holmes. Of course, you may keep that copy and apply your decoding skills to it if you wish. I assume that you possess such skills, do you not?"

"I assure you, Minister, that my skills are every bit as up to snuff as those of your staff."

"Ah, splendid. I shall be eager to hear from you."

We departed and walked back to the hotel.

"Really, Holmes, I never knew that you had studied code-breaking. You never cease to amaze me."

"I know absolutely nothing about it."

"But you just told the Minister ..."

"I told him I had the same level of skills as his staff, and that, I am quite certain, is the truth."

Chapter Ten   Down By the Bay

telegram from the Minister was delivered to Holmes the following morning. It read:

MR. HOLMES: AS YOUR ITINERARY SHOWS THAT YOU WILL MAKE A CIRCUIT OF TOKYO BAY THIS COMING WEEK, KINDLY MAKE INQUIRIES CONCERNING OUR MISSING ATTACHÉ, SEAN O'NEILL. HIS DISAPPEARANCE IS LIKELY RELATED TO THE FILE I GAVE YOU. WE ARE COUNTING ON YOU. HUMPHREY.

Two days later, we began a circumnavigation of Tokyo Bay, stopping at towns in Chiba, and then taking the ferry across from Tateyama to the island of Oshima. I was quite taken up with the local customs, food, flowers, and history. I even took time out to climb to the top of the Mount Mihara volcano crater on Oshima.

Holmes, on the other hand, was lost in thought, delivering his lectures almost mechanically. As soon as he was free of official functions, he retreated to his room and yet again opened the file regarding Mrs. Munro.

"Your thoughts, please, Watson," he said to me as we stood at the rail of the ferry while it crossed the mouth of Tokyo Bay from the island of Oshima to the port of Ito on the Izu Peninsula. I should have obliged him by talking about the missing attaché, but my thoughts were entirely elsewhere. I was looking out to the western horizon. As the morning mists cleared, the massive, awesome cone of Mount Fuji appeared at the edge of the world. It must have been over one hundred miles away, but it towered over the rest of the landscape. "My goodness, Holmes, I gasped. Is that not one of the most magnificent sites of nature you have ever seen?"

Holmes raised his gaze briefly to the horizon and then returned to his notes.

"Kindly leave you wonderment to later, Watson. Right now, I need your attention to the matters at hand. Now then, this is what we know so far."

I sighed, gave a parting look in adoration to the sacred mountain, and began to listen to Holmes's recitation of the data to date.

"It has been suggested to us that there might be some connection to the disappearance of this O'Neill fellow to the international conflict and intrigue that has beset this corner of the globe for the past two years. I have put my mind to work on this for several days, yet task it mightily as I can, I am not able to see any logical connection. The little island of Oshima has no more than a few fishing boats and a commendable school or two. The towns we are making our way to are famous for their hot springs and serve primarily as vacation spots for the Japanese people of modest means and foreign visitors. Rather like Brighton without the monstrous pier. All of the ports and islands that are the cause of conflict with the Russians are on the other side of the country. What could this pleasant little region possibly offer to anyone? Flowers, fish, and public baths may all be enjoyable parts of Japanese life, but strategically there is nothing to be gained. What think you, doctor?"

Holmes was yet again asking my thoughts and opinions on crimes and mysteries that he was working on. On this occasion, however, I did have a thought. I had spent several years in Her Majesty's Expeditionary Forces and had learned a thing or two about military strategy. So, with some confidence, I offered my opinion.

"I have observed," I said, "that the greater area of Tokyo and Yokohama appears to be the beating heart of the country, the sole center of all commerce, finance, trade, and political control."

"Yes, Watson, that has been obvious. The hinterland is still somewhat primitive by comparison. Go on."

"Well then, if I had been the Czar or the poor chap who was Admiral of his Baltic Fleet, I would never have sailed through the East China Sea and into the Sea of Japan. Port Arthur had already fallen, and he sailed into a trap. The boats were spotted, and the Japanese Navy was ready and waiting for him. If I had been in charge, I would have sailed east into the Pacific and then swung back and charged into Tokyo Bay and blockaded it. The hundreds of trading ships that enter and leave this body of water could have been bottled up. Japanese commerce would be brought to an ignominious halt. Yes, I would have used the same strategy as Admiral Perry did fifty years ago. It worked then. It might have worked again. That is what I think, Holmes."

"Ah, interesting, doctor. But what has that to do with our Mr. O'Neill."

"If he were in cahoots with the Russians, then he could have sent back all the intelligence necessary regarding what harbors to use, what straits to be avoided, and what ships of the Japanese Navy were nearby."

Holmes said nothing for several minutes and continued to look out to sea.

"I must say, Watson, that is a rather good deduction. Yes, rather good, indeed. Had he provided good intelligence to the Russians, and had they followed your strategy, the war might have taken a very different turn. That, however, we shall never know, but it does help us to narrow our search for the chap to those avenues that might have been of interest to a spy. Thank you, Watson. That has been very useful."

Such praise from Holmes was rare, and I confess that my chest puffed up just a little. I began to fix my gaze on the approaching coastline, looking for strategic harbors into which Russian battleships should have sailed and in which the attaché might still be hiding.

"I made some inquiries," said Holmes as we neared the port, "concerning our lost attaché. He was seen on the island, but it was agreed that he departed on the same boat that we are now on. The island is a small place with a tightly knit populace. It is impossible that our attaché could have returned there and hidden himself. For that reason, and given your insights concerning the necessity of intelligence information, I fully suspect that he is still hiding in one of these towns along the edge of the bay. As it is always easier to hide in a larger center than a smaller one, I am conjecturing that we might manage to run into Mr. O'Neill in Atami. Would you agree?"

I immediately agreed, although I must admit I had no idea where the blighter might have gone. He could be halfway to Timbuktu by now, for all I knew.

Our lectures in the towns of the peninsula went well. The crowds were smaller and poorer than we found in the capital of Tokyo, but that was to be expected. After the lecture in Atami, Holmes took me aside.

"Even though I do not trust our Tommy farther than I could throw him, he has been quite helpful in asking discreet questions about the missing British diplomat. He has been seen around this town on numerous occasions, and Tommy believes that he may be residing at one of the most exclusive retreats in the upper town, beyond the railway tracks. I have asked him to arrange a visit for us to the place. I assume, doctor, that you are prepared to participate in an *onsen?*"

I had read briefly about Japan's public baths. Atami had an abundance of them since the warm mineral water that the people prized so greatly was bubbling up from the depths in many places within the townsite.

"I am game, Holmes, if you are."

Excellent, Watson. It will be a superb cultural adventure for us."

"Oh, Sherlock-san, that is wonderful news," said Tommy beaming and bowing. "You will enjoy the onsen very much. The onsen in Atami are *sandaionsen,* one of Japan's three great hot springs. The Japanese people have enjoyed them for over seven hundred years. I will make all arrangements. You will enjoy them very much. They are famous for refreshing both the body and soul."

I was not all convinced that my soul needed refreshing, but a good long soak in a warm bath could do my body no harm. So, the following day we took a cab from the lower town up to the Baien Park where we were let off.

"It is unfortunate," said Tommy, "that you could not be here back in February when the plum blossoms were blooming. They are not so abundant as the cherry blossoms, but they are fragrant. The experience is very good for the refreshing both the senses and the soul."

As it seemed inevitable that, in spite of my lack of appropriate motivation, my soul was to be attended to, I smiled at Tommy and made my way up the paths through the park. At the far end, perched on the top of the hill was a sprawling building. We entered and were immediately greeted by several beautiful young women, all dressed in kimonos and all with facial make-up that lightened their complexions. They took our shoes from us and led us through a sliding door and into an inner portion of the complex.

"I have arranged a private washing area, sirs," said Tommy. "The price is more, but you are special gaijin visitors, and it would not do to have you treated like ordinary bathers. You will enjoy. Please remove your clothes and give them to the attendant."

"Please, Tommy," I asked, "where are the baths? All I can see inside these cubicles is a stool."

"Ah, yes, Doctor John-san. This is where you are washed. Your body must be clean before entering the bath. Your helper will be here soon to wash you. Please remove your clothes and have a seat on the stool."

I shrugged and did as I was told. A few moments later, the door to my cubicle opened, and I turned to see who was joining me. I gasped and blushed. The helper was another beautiful young woman in a kimono. She was bearing a large bucket of water in her one hand and some implements, soap, and brushes in her other. She bowed graciously and smiled, saying some words in Japanese that were incomprehensible. She put the bucket on the floor and, using a large dipper, extracted a quart or so of water, smiled again, and poured it over my head.

The water was startlingly hot and aromatic, with strong vapors of minerals invading my nostrils. The young woman then proceeded to scrub, rather more vigorously than I considered necessary, every square inch of my epidermis. When she was done, she smiled and bowed again and departed. A moment later, the door was opened by Tommy, who stood entirely naked except for a towel that he held in a strategic location.

"Come now, Dr. John-san. We can go to the bath."

When is Rome, do as the Romans do, is a well-known adage, and I assumed that it applied equally in Japan. So I held my towel in a discreet manner and followed him. I could see Holmes following us, his hands and towel similarly positioned. We followed Tommy out of the washing area and through another sliding door into a large moisture-laden hall in which I could see a pool of water waiting for us. Again, I stopped short and felt my eyes nearly pop out of my head. In the room must have been at least a hundred people *of both sexes,* mostly in the same age span of life as Holmes and me, and all as unclad as the day they were born. Good heavens, I thought to myself, this would never do in England, not even in Bath do they bathe in such a manner.

It was disconcerting enough to follow Tommy to the edge of the pool while grasping firmly to my towel, but the word had gone out, it seemed, that two famous gaijin were visiting the onsen, and no end of men and women accosted me, smiled, bowed, and gave a friendly greeting. I would have preferred that they not bowed slowly and deeply while standing directly in front of my towel.

Once in the near-scalding water, I slowly relaxed, placed my folded towel on the top of my head, closed my eyes, and enjoyed the aromas and the overwhelming sensory pleasure to which I had succumbed. Holmes did the same. When I opened my eyes, I was startled to see another European face sitting directly across from me and looking at me.

"Hello there, old chap," spoke the fellow. "Nice to have you come and visit. I was told that you boys were looking for me. So very kind of you to be concerned for my well-being. I can assure you, however, that I am alive and well and living in Atami."

Holmes calmly replied, "Attaché O'Neill, I presume."

"At your service, Mr. Sherlock Holmes. I must say that as one of your fans, I have always dreamed of chatting with you someday, but I must admit, really sir, that I never imagined with a towel instead of your famous hat on your head." He chuckled pleasantly.

"I do so wish I could stay and converse with the two of you, but I'm afraid that I am frightfully busy. My new enterprise here is enriching my bank account at ten times the rate I was paid by His Majesty's Treasury. And, if I may say so, such a business is a pleasure. So many grateful customers, especially visitors from eastern Europe, where they do love their baths and thoroughly enjoy the enlightened way of doing things in this part of Nippon. So, terribly sorry there, old chaps, but I must excuse myself. Business calls. Give my regards to the Legation."

He immediately stood up and departed the bath, leaving us to stare at the pale, flabby, and pock-marked display of Irish buttocks.

I jumped up immediately to follow him, dislodging my towel as I did so. I instinctively fetched it out of the water and began to wring it out as I sloshed my way to the edge of the pool. Tommy jumped toward me and grabbed my arm.

"No, Dr. John-san. You must not wring out your towel in the bath. This is very impolite and not acceptable etiquette. Please, sir, sit down, and I will get you a dry one."

"But we must follow that man. We have to speak to him." I watched as the attaché walked along the far side of the pool and opened a door on the wall opposite to the one from which we had entered.

"Dr. John-san, you cannot go into that room. It is, how do you say in English, *for members only*. You must be invited and approved by the owners of the onsen. It would not be safe just to walk in. They have *bodyguards*."

"Then we must call the police." I blustered.

"Oh, Doctor-san, that would be very difficult for the police. It is very bad manners to interfere in the private affairs of an exclusive onsen. It is not good for the police to do such a thing."

"Good heavens, Tommy. What in the world goes on back there that is worthy of such respect?"

"Ah, respect, you say, Doctor John-san. That is very kind of you. I cannot say for sure, sir, but it is possible that your friend is providing very, shall we say, *pleasurable* services for visiting gaijin. They pay very dearly for the private space and the provision of *onsen geisha* and, of course, excellent sake and shochu. They are good business, as you say, for the onsen, and for the town."

I resumed my seat in the water and looked over at Holmes.

"Elementary, Watson. Out attaché just staged a very clever event. Quite brilliant of him, I must say. We now know that he is alive and well and are obligated to duly report same, but he has protected himself very astutely. He can carry on confidential, private conversations with his European clients, allow them to indulge in the exotic pleasures of the Orient, and be protected by the police and his bodyguards. I would wager that he has an army of Japanese informants among the employees of this establishment who report to him on the comings and goings and overheard conversations of every foreigner who risks and hazards all he hath by entering this place. My grudging respect to him. Frankly, there might be a lesson to be learned here for the future operations of Baker Street."

I pondered Holmes's words and concluded that he must surely be jesting about Baker Street.

Chapter Eleven   The Blue Ribbon

By the time we returned to Tokyo in early June, the time for the second athletic contest had arrived. We were briefed on our role by the Second Minister and, in turn passed along what we had learned during our journey along the coast of the bay.

On the fifteenth of June, we boarded a crowded train and traveled a few miles to the Takeaosangushi station. This was the start point of the next race, the ten-mile run that began with the ascent of the two thousand foot Mount Takeo, and then continued with the run up and down through the forest all the way to the top of Mount Jinba. The paths were narrow, and the officials started the two hundred men in heats. I took notice, as did Holmes, of the Russian teacher amongst them. Once the men had all departed, the women were lined up. Yet again, I could not help but wonder at the diminutive size of most of them. Except for a handful of younger women, none was more than a hairsbreadth over five feet. It was amazing, I thought, that such small women could bounce up the rocks and steps that they would have to navigate over the next three hours.

Once all the runners were dispatched, Tommy led us to a row of carriages.

"Now we go to the place where the race ends. We must be there to greet the winners."

The carriage rambled quickly along a narrow road through the valleys and then let us off at a point a short distance from the Hachiman Shrine.

"From here we walk," said Tommy, smiling as always.

I distinctly remember hearing him say *walk,* and not *climb.* The fellow was entirely misleading. For the next hour, we grunted and gasped as we ascended a steep path through the pine forest. Had I been able to catch my breath, it might have been a pleasant outing. By the time we arrived at the summit of Mount Jinba, nearly three thousand feet above the level of Tokyo, I was drenched with sweat and decided that I had set a tax upon my legs sufficient for the next year.

"Ah, we are most fortunate," exulted Tommy. "Many days, the view from the top of the mountain is not clear, and all that can be seen is the inside of a cloud. But today is a perfect day for enjoying the beauty."

Having caught my breath and cooled off, I looked at the magnificent natural spectacle in front of me. For a full three hundred and sixty degrees, I could observe the hills of Japan. Quite pleasant, I had to agree.

Holmes had said little either on the way up or once we reached the summit. As an inveterate user of tobacco, he had filled his lungs with all those nasty things that made hiking up mountains a less than delightful pastime. Inwardly, I smirked and thought that this would teach him a good lesson, although the likelihood of his reforming his habits was negligible. After several minutes of recovering, he finally began to chat. His mind was not on the beautiful prospect.

"I am eager to see how our Russian runner does. I would not be at all surprised to see him finish well back of the winner but sufficiently forward to make the cut. Just as he did the last time."

If the Russian, as is common to their breed, consumed as much vodka and tobacco as every other Russian I had ever met, I would not be at all surprised if he never made it to the finish line.

Soon a crowd of nearly one hundred people had gathered at the summit. Several tents had been pitched, and refreshments were offered at a price that could be considered larceny. Our envoy, who would soon be an ambassador, and his statuesque wife appeared wearing stylish sporting clothes appropriate for climbing small mountains.

Tommy sat beside us and kept checking his watch.

"The leading men should be here very soon. Then they will check the times at which their heat was started and announce the winners."

"And what," asked Holmes, "is the reward for the winners?"

"The winners will receive their kimonos and medals, but only the first forty men and the first twenty women will be allowed to enter the final contest. All of the others will be content with the pride that goes with having completed a very difficult task."

"Why," I asked, incredulously, "would the stragglers even bother to finish then, if they get nothing from it."

Tommy gave me a strange look, somewhat aghast. "Doctor-san, to be in a race like this and then not to finish would bring dishonor to your family and to your name. A young man could not dare to have such a failure attached to his name for the rest of his life. They will all finish the race, Doctor-san, even if they have to crawl to the finish line."

The first chaps to appear on the trail below the summit were certainly not crawling. They were moving upwards in leaps and bounds, scampering over rocks and taking steps two or three at a time. I could not help but think that if recruited for Oxford and turned into proper Englishman, they would be brilliant additions to our team at the Olympics.

As the front-runners approached the finish line, the crowd gave polite applause, and the press snapped off their pictures. Various people came forward bearing kimonos for them so that, unlike the chaps in the onsen, their limbs would be modestly covered. The race having started in heats, however, there was no way of knowing yet who the winner was. The real cheering would be reserved for that fellow once he was announced.

Over the next hour, the male runners continued to appear, some the picture of robust good health and others giving evidence of a lack of sufficient training. As we approached the hour and a quarter mark since the first runner had crossed, Tommy excitedly announced, "The women are just below us. The first one to cross will be the winner."

The one in the lead I immediately recognized. She was the same tiny thing that had won the race around the Palace. She bounded toward the finish line, and for a brief few seconds, before she was covered in a robe, I looked at her petite body. She was no longer young, but there was not an ounce of fat on it, and the muscles and sinews were sharply defined. I was fairly certain that she had been running every day of her life for the past decade. She received a well-deserved heartily round of applause.

What was not surprising to me was the arrival close behind her of some of the taller, young teenage women. Their long legs would have given them a distinct advantage on the rocks and steps. They were likewise given robes and glasses of cold water by their friends and the officials.

A full hour passed until the last of the runners had crossed the line. I was pleased to see that Envoy Grant and his wife greeted every one of them, exchanged polite bows, and presented them with a small printed card, bearing a citation from His Majesty, as well as a tiny Union Jack, stapled to a thin foot of doweling. Mrs. Munro stood for some time chatting in Japanese with the winning woman, and then I could see her surrounded by some of the younger girls. I assumed that she was no doubt encouraging their continued emancipation. Not surprising was her one-on-one brief conversation with the Russian, who had managed, as Holmes had predicted, to finish within the limit of the cut for the final race.

The officials huddled together, going over the time lists. A piece of paper was then handed to the race official who stood and, beginning with the runner in tenth place, called out first the winners of the women's race, and followed that with the winners among the men. A great cheer went up as the winning man and woman came forward and politely bowed. As they did so, Sherlock Holmes reached out his long arms, bearing a thick blue ribbon, with a medallion attached. With an unfeigned smile, he hung them around their necks. The press were all over the place, snapping photographs of the event. It was, I thought, jolly good publicity for the Empire.

"Mr. Holmes, Dr. Watson," said the elegant Mrs. Munro to the two of us once all the ceremonies were over. "I am so sorry that we cannot invite you across the street this time for a pleasant lunch. But we are holding a reception in three days at the Legation for the winners, and you simply must attend. It just would not be the same without you. The Japanese are all on fire to learn more about you." She smiled warmly and touched the forearms of first Holmes and then me as she spoke.

"If I were them," answered Holmes, "I would be more on fire to learn about you, Mrs. Munro."

She responded with a merry peal of laughter. "My goodness, Mr. Holmes, I dare say you are trying to be charming. How thoughtful of you. I shall so look forward to seeing you again soon."

The reception was the type of stuffy affair that my friend, Sherlock Holmes, detests. We had to dress up in formal attire in spite of the now warm and humid weather. Both of us were accosted throughout the evening by gaijin and Japanese, and endlessly asked the same questions. If either of us had to respond one more time to those who claimed to have been wonderfully terrified at the thought of an enormous hound, I am quite sure we would have howled at the moon and run off into the darkness.

The winners of both the men's and the women's races were all present, now splendidly attired in their traditional kimonos. What surprised me as I looked over the crowd was the presence of Miss Esther Biddle, the Headmistress of the Quaker School for Girls. Beside her, and chatting amiably, were the Russian, Mr. Lobachevesky, and Mrs. Munro. As the headmistress had not been at the race at all and the Russian had only placed among those who made the cut and not among the winners, it seemed odd that they would be present. My curiosity got the better of me, and I approached them.

"Miss Biddle," I said, with as warm a smile as I could feign. "Such a pleasant surprise to see you here. I would never have guessed that you might be interested in elite athletics. Were you a runner yourself in your youth?"

She laughed at my pleasantry. "Why hello, Dr. Watson, you know the girls are all still talking about your visit. And no, doctor, I was anything but a runner in my distant youth. But our team placed first in the last race, didn't we, Nick?" She addressed the question to the Russian, who was standing beside her.

"Yah, that we do. Three girls from out team finish in first twenty runners. We are proud of them."

"So that is why we were invited, Doctor. Our girls did us proud. And don't you agree that they clean up wonderfully and look beautiful in their kimonos?" She gestured with her hand to the crowd. Every Japanese woman present was wearing a kimono, had her hair bundled up on top of her head, and frankly, I had a difficult time telling one from the next. I guessed that some of the tall younger ones might have been her students, but beyond that, I was at a complete loss.

"They look," I said, "utterly lovely. I am sure you are very proud of them."

We chatted for a few more minutes during which I told the story, in a self-effacing manner of our escapade in the onsen in Atami. I refrained, of course, from any reference to Mr. O'Neill.

They all laughed loudly at my description of Holmes and me clutching our towels for dear life.

In response, Mrs. Munro said, "I go several times a year down to Atami. It is such a fun place to visit. The waiters and the hotel staff all speak a bit of English, and an afternoon out on one of the boats in the harbor is as relaxing as anything I have ever experienced in New Jersey."

It occurred to me that she had not set the bar very high in her comparison, but I refrained from drawing this to her attention and made a note to myself to pass what I had just heard along to Holmes.

While we were still chatting, a chap from the embassy assumed the role of *majordomo* and called the gathering to order. For the next half hour, we stood and listened to yet more short speeches by Envoy Grant, by a chap representing British firms operating in Japan, and by their counterparts from the Japanese government. The details of the final race were confirmed. A full scholarship to Oxford would be awarded by His Majesty and the Emperor himself had agreed to be present at the finish line. He would give one of the most prestigious awards within the culture and history of Japan, an arrow made of pure gold, to the winners. One would be awarded to the victorious man and one to the woman.

I leaned my head to Miss Biddle and whispered, "Is the Emperor going to climb Mount Fuji?"

"No," she whispered back. "He gets carried. But the rest of us will have to climb. I've done it twice before, and I can promise you, doctor, it is a joy to get to the summit, but it is far from easy."

As soon as the formalities were over, I felt Holmes's hand on my arm.

"Unless you have some very good reason for remaining here, my friend, I do ask that we leave straight away."

"In full agreement," I assured him.

As we walked back to the Legation, I passed along to Holmes what I had learned from my conversation with Mrs. Munro.

"Thank you, Watson, that data is most useful. There is obviously a collusion that has taken place and connects all of the suspicious activities that I have been made aware of—the murder of the American, Mr. Boulanger, the strange disappearances of Mrs. Munro, and the equally inexplicable transactions in her bank account, the illicit connection to the Russian teacher, the self-imposed local exile of the attaché, and the British athletic events. They all are connected in some way, and Mrs. Munro is at the center of it all. They are clearly up to something, but, so far, I am at a loss to deduce what in the devil it is they are planning. Any thoughts, Watson?"

"Not the foggiest notion, Holmes."

"As I expected."

Chapter Twelve
A Revelation While South

The final leg of our lecture tour would take us west and south to the cities of Nagoya, Kyoto, Osaka, Kobe, Hiroshima, and eventually all the way to Nagasaki on the north-eastern corner of the island of Kyushu. Along the way, we would stop at several other smaller centers and, when it was all over, return by ferry to Tokyo. For the next three weeks, we would have no choice but to put Mrs. Munro and her clandestine Russian connections out of our minds and enjoy the natural beauty, the fascinating history, and the warm welcome afforded us by this unique nation. I was determined to do just that. Holmes was equally determined not to. He delivered his lecture in a diligent, professional manner, but I could tell that his brilliant mind was elsewhere, never taking a rest from rolling back and forth over all the data of this puzzling case. He politely tolerated the effusive welcomes of the local people in each place and, if he could not find an excuse to bow out, visited all the nearby shrines, temples, and wonders of nature.

I had to admit, that by the end of the three weeks, I had come to the conclusion that, just like Scottish castles and ancient oak trees, once you have seen one ancient Buddhist temple or sparkling waterfall, you have seen them all. While sleeping on the floor on a *tatami* mat and a thin mattress might be fine for these Oriental chaps, I had gotten tired of waking up with sore shoulders and hips.

A telegram from the Second Minister, Redvers Humphrey, brought our peaceful sojourn on Kyushu to an abrupt halt. It arrived during our final week as we enjoyed the unspoiled natural beauty of the island. Holmes read it, assumed a very perplexed countenance, and handed it on to me. It ran:

> HOLMES: BELOW, LATEST MESSAGE INTERCEPTED FROM MRS. EKATERINA FEDEROV-MUNRO. YOUR ATTENTION TO THIS MATTER MOST PRESSING. PLEASE CONTACT ME IMMEDIATELY UPON RETURN TO TOKYO. HUMPHREY.

Любимая моя:

> Only a few more weeks until your triumphal ascent to the peak of Mount Fuji. How you will astonish them, Ангел мой, with your courage and determination. Your accomplishment forever will be a source of pride to your country.
>
> You, my child of the moon who has grown into the most beautiful of human beings; you have already vanquished the princes and sent them packing. It is only the Emperor himself who remains. He will give you the golden arrow, but with it, you will break his heart. And then the heavens will take you home.
>
> I have believed in you since the day you entered my life. I will believe in you always. I will be waiting for you at the summit of the sacred mountain to watch you receive the golden arrow and the bright yellow ribbon around your neck. As he bestows these upon you, the Emperor will be closer to you than He ever is to any of his people. Make the time last forever in your memory, in mine, and in all the struggling people of the world.
>
> Моё сердце полно любви
>
> Your Effie.

Other than the unseemly nature of a married woman writing deeply passionate notes to a lover, I could make nothing of the contents, except that she was encouraging him to win the final race and might even have believed that he could.

For the next ten minutes, Holmes read and re-read the letter. Then, as was his cherished habit, he sat back, closed his eyes, and brought his hands and fingertips together. For another ten minutes, I watched his lips move ever so slightly, and his head shake from side to side as he carried on a disciplined, rational argument inside his mind.

Then his hands suddenly dropped, and his eyes popped wide open.

"Good Lord, Watson. They are planning the unthinkable. It's all in the messages. It all fits together. Good Lord, the consequences would be disastrous. Calamitous. Not just for Britain and Japan, but for the whole world."

"Merciful heavens, Holmes," I sputtered. "What are you talking about? What are they going to do?"

"If Lobachevesky wins the race, he will be presented directly to Emperor, will he not?"

"Yes, that is what is expected."

"He will kneel in front of the Emperor, and the golden arrow will be placed in his outstretched hands. Correct?"

"Yes. I suppose so. But what of it?"

"Oh, dear God, Watson. Can you not see? He is going to assassinate the Emperor."

I was speechless. Fear trembled through my body at what Holmes had just said.

"No. He would never do such a thing. How could he?"

"With the arrow, Watson. In less than a second, he could turn it and plunge the tip directly into the heart of the Emperor. No one is even close enough to do any harm, but he will be. He has long, powerful arms. He and his lover are the only Russians still at large in Tokyo. They will wreak revenge for the defeat of their navy. They will prove that they are the true victors of the war. Disaster will follow. Japan will invade Russia in retaliation. The French are allied with the Russians. The Germans and Austrian are friendly to the Japanese. We could end up in Armageddon."

"Holmes," I said, "are you sure?"

"Good heavens, Watson. No, of course, I am not sure. How could anyone be certain? The data is confusing and coded. We have yet to decipher the message in code. It is always dangerous to jump to a conclusion with insufficient information. But what little we know is clearly pointing us to a probable outcome that would be terrible beyond words."

He sat in silence, and I did the same, gripping the arms of the chair until my knuckles had turned white.

"What," I whispered, "are you going to do? Can you report your fears to Humphrey?"

"No. The time has long past when we can make use of that pompous blowhard. No, Watson. The time has come for us to bring the evidence directly to Mr. Grant Munro and force him to face up to the duplicity, the *treason* of his wife. I shall request an emergency meeting immediately upon our return."

"We have only the one remaining lecture before we head back. Do you think you can manage?"

"I will do my best. We must not give any hint that we are on to anything. Maintaining normal behavior is imperative."

True to his word, Holmes delivered an energetic lecture, dwelling perhaps more than usual on accounts of people who had been in positions of trust and who so violated it by their nefarious actions. We retired to our hotel, and I went to bed immediately, knowing that our morning would start early.

It began, I must say, even earlier than expected. At four o'clock, I felt Holmes hand on my shoulder.

"Come, Watson. The game is afoot. Please rise, get ready, and come with me to the station."

"Goodness gracious, Holmes. We have four hours before the train leaves for the port. What is your rush?"

"I have not slept. This miserable hotel suite is too small to provide room to pace and think. The platform of the station is much better. Please, come at once."

I staggered from my bed, bathed quickly, dressed and packed. Within twenty minutes, Holmes and I were out of our rooms and standing at the door of the hotel waiting for a cab to the station.

"What about, Tommy? What will he do?" I asked.

"He will get up at a reasonable hour, find us already departed, have a heart attack, and come running to the station. What do you think he will do?"

As predicted, Holmes spent the next two hours pacing back and forth along the station platform while I tried to scribble some notes. At the twenty-minute mark before our train's departure, I saw Tommy appear at the far end of the platform and come running pell-mell in our direction. His face was beet red, and the sweat was dripping off his brow.

"Good morning, Tommy," I said cheerfully. "We were much too excited about our return to Tokyo to sleep, so we came a bit early. It would have been terribly inconsiderate of us not to let you sleep. I do hope you slept well."

"Yes, Dr. John-san, quite well. It is only that I did not wake up well. I was very worried that something had happened to you and Sherlock-san."

"Oh, come, come, Tommy. Where could we possibly go? Our sole destination is the station. The train is the only way to the port."

"Ah yes, doctor-san, you are right."

I felt sorry for the poor chap. I had become rather fond of him. He was invariably well-dressed, perfectly mannered, and entirely conscientious in carrying out his assigned tasks. Some mornings he seemed bleary-eyed, and I wondered what mischief he, being a young man, might have gotten up to late at night and far away from his home city. On many of our train journeys, he, like so many other young Japanese men, fell fast asleep, waking just in time not to miss the station where they had to get off.

The train took us across the island and over to the port of Kitakyushi. There we boarded the ferry to Tokyo. It would be a full two-day journey. Fortunately, it was a large domestic ferry, and the deck provided Holmes with ample room to pace back and forth. The seas were calm, and the weather, although damp, was warm and otherwise tolerable.

Upon our return to the harbor of Tokyo in the evening of the following day, we took a cab directly to the hotel. Holmes had sent a telegram already to the Office of the Envoy, and a reply from the Legation was waiting for us at the Imperial Hotel. Holmes ripped it open while he stood at the front desk.

"Excellent. It appears that our envoy will leave Tokyo in three days to travel to Singapore for a meeting. In order to accommodate my request, he has granted us an hour tomorrow morning at eleven. So, Watson, if you would not mind, please review all of your notes and have them ready for presentation. I will do likewise."

I would do so for a few hours and then would get some sleep. Holmes, indefatigable as always, would not sleep at all and would spend the entire night rehearsing the words he would say the following day, making sure that he had all his facts in order as he confronted Mr. Grant Munro with the unpleasant news of his wife's unfaithfulness and treachery.

At breakfast the following morning, Holmes ate little and said nothing. During the walk from the hotel to the Legation, he was likewise silent but quickening his pace. Having known and watched him closely now for a quarter-century, I could tell that he was tightly wound up inside. I knew that inside his head, the meeting we were about to take part in was being played out in every possible dialogue imaginable.

"My dear friend," I said. "Try to relax. Calm yourself. Think about something else. Think about England; about Regent Park, or Scotland Yard. Anything other than what is bringing turmoil to your soul."

He gave me a scornful look. "You, of all people, Watson, should know that what you ask is beyond impossible. It is ridiculous. Kindly desist."

He was right. I knew my efforts at cajoling were a waste of time. I said no more.

Chapter Thirteen   The Truth Hurts

"Ah, Mr. Sherlock Holmes and Dr. Watson," enthused Envoy Munro as we were shown into his office. "So good to see you. I have heard splendid reports of your lectures throughout the country. Lovely of you to come and report in so promptly."

"I regret," said Holmes, "having to insist on an immediate meeting."

"Not at all. Not at all, my good chap. The timing is perfect. I shall be leaving in two days for Singapore. Whitehall has called a special council of its agents in this part of the world, and I am compelled to attend."

"Oh, dear," I said. "Why, you will miss the final athletic event. The one for the yellow ribbon."

"Yes, Doctor Watson, I'm afraid I shall. Frightfully disappointing and all. But it seems that at this meeting, the elevation of our legation to a full embassy will be made official, and I suppose that I shall be invested as the ambassador. So it is best that I show up."

"Of course," I said. "And I believe that congratulations are in order. Henceforth you will be His Excellency, the Ambassador. Congratulations, indeed, Mr. Munro."

"Yes," added Holmes. "Our congratulations."

"Oh, thank you. Both of you. You are being very kind and generous. But the truth, as I am sure you know, is that I had nothing whatsoever to do with it. It is all because of the thorough thumping the Japs gave to the Ruskies. Had they lost the war, this office would have remained a lowly legation for several more years. The Japanese press and the boys over at the Diet have already started calling our office an Embassy and me the Ambassador, but that it only because our promotion is a feather in their cap. Officially, I am still an Envoy in charge of a Legation until several days hence. But Fortune does what she will, and I am a most fortunate man."

"Congratulations all the same," I said. Holmes, sensing the futility of the current course of the conversation, brought it to a sharp stop.

"Mr. Munro," he said, looking directly at the envoy. "I fear that our report may cause you to change your cheerful opinion of your good fortune."

Mr. Munro shut down his smile and looked directly back at Holmes. "Is that so, Mr. Holmes? Very well, then, please be seated and deliver your report. I am all attention."

He sat behind his large desk and Holmes and I in chairs in front of it. Holmes began his account and would work his way up from the less important to the utterly devastating in impeccable and logical order.

"Permit me to begin," said Holmes, "with the matters of lesser concern."

"Begin wherever you wish, Mr. Holmes."

"Very well. You should be aware that the young man who was provided to us, the one named Toshi or Tommy, is a spy. I have good reason to believe that he is informing on us, and I need to make you aware of that."

The Envoy responded with a blank look on his face.

"Of course, he is informing on you Mr. Holmes. I pay him jolly good money to inform on you, and so does the Office of the Prime Minister of Japan. Every night the lad writes up a report first in Japanese and then in English and makes sure that it is delivered to the correct desk by ten o'clock the following morning. Surely you don't think that the world's most famous detective and England's most popular writer were going to prance all over these islands without our knowing every place you went, every person you met, every word you said, and that was said to you, every blessed thing you ate for breakfast, lunch and dinner. Tommy has exceeded our expectations in his job. Quite the brilliant young man. That's why we got him a Rhodes and sent him off to Oxford for two years."

He paused and shook his head before calmly assuming a practiced diplomatic posture.

"The next items on your list of concerns, Mr. Holmes. Please"

Holmes likewise retained a passive face, although I knew that behind it, he did not like what had just taken place.

"I assume," Holmes responded, "that your Second Minister, Mr. Redvers Humphrey, informed you that I had tracked down your missing cultural attaché?"

I observed a very slight twitch in the Envoy's face. I guessed that his Minister had not so informed him. But he smiled and spoke in a carefully measured tone.

"No, Mr. Holmes. He is a rather busy chap and has not yet had the opportunity to make that report. So why don't you just go ahead and do it for him."

Holmes then gave a detailed account of our successful efforts during our journey from Oshima to Atami. He left out any reference to towels.

"On the basis of what we have uncovered," he continued, with no pun intended, "I have deduced that the most reasonable conclusion to draw is that your attaché has become a turncoat and is now engaged in clandestine espionage activities with agents from

Eastern Europe. All of them, as I am sure you would agree, all are in direct contact with the regime of the Czar."

Mr. Munro tilted his head and smiled ever so slightly.

"You did say, did you not Mr. Holmes, that he has set up operations in the private section of an exclusive onsen in Atami?"

"I did."

"And that he has been known to bring in guests who are obviously Poles, or Ukrainians, or Bulgarians and so forth and to make sure that they are provided with copious amounts of sake and the companionship of an onsen geisha."

"You are repeating what I have told you, Envoy."

"Oh, yes. Yes. I guess I am. Pardon me. But permit me to ask you, Mr. Holmes, do you know the difference between a *geisha* and an *onsen geisha*?"

Holmes looked a little perplexed but, in keeping with his character, was frank and forthcoming.

"No, Envoy Munro, I do not."

"Then allow me to add some data to your brilliant mind, Mr. Holmes. A *geisha* is a highly respected and educated woman who has trained for years to be a musician, an artist, and above all, a skilled and informed conversationalist who provides excellent company for a Japanese gentleman. An *onsen geisha* is not a *geisha*. She is a prostitute. A cut above those that inhabit the streets of the East End, perhaps, but a prostitute all the same. What you have just told me, Mr. Holmes, is not that my attaché has become a spy but that he has become a bloody pimp."

The last words were spoken through a face that was struggling to contain laughter. Now the Envoy broke into a merry chuckle.

"However, Mr. Holmes, please do not think that I am ungrateful for the information. I will so inform Whitehall and list him as having resigned and move ahead with finding his replacement. Thank you, Mr. Holmes. Now, what is next on your list?"

If Holmes was disconcerted by that exchange, he again did not show it. He carried on.

"You already have my report on the dead American fellow who ended up in the river, do you not?"

"I do. Now that was indeed very helpful. It gave me a delightful one-upmanship opportunity with my American counterpart. I do thank you for that one. Is there something else you need to tell me about that?"

"What I deliberately left out of the report was the name of the Russian agent who was making the sales. His name was General Federov."

Mr. Munro looked puzzled.

"You mean Yaroslav Federov? That fellow? Who else could it be?"

"You know this man?" Holmes asked.

"Of course, I know him. He's in charge of all sorts of the buying and selling of arms and armaments for the Russians. Our fine British arms manufacturers have sold him millions of pounds worth of rifles, bombs, grenades ... you name it. One of our best customers. Why in the world, Mr. Holmes, would you think it necessary to withhold his name from your report?"

"I did so," said Holmes, sounding not entirely sure of himself, "because he bears the same family name as your wife."

Yet again, Mr. Munro looked at Holmes and shook his head. "Are you telling me, Mr. Holmes, that you suspect that there is some sort of familial connection between my wife and General Federov?"

"That is always a possibility that cannot be ruled out?"

A smile of condescension bordering on contempt swept across the Envoy's face. "I take it, Mr. Holmes, that you have never been to

Russia. Yes, I can see by the look on your face that you have not. So let me enlighten you, Mr. Holmes, you have just claimed that two individuals who both bear the names of Smith, or Johnson, or Brown or Williams must be in familial collusion with each other. That is what you are suspecting and that, Mr. Holmes is absurd. Federov is one of the most common names in Russia. There must be half a million of them. Yaroslav Federov is from Novgorod, and my wife's family is from Vladivostok. They are over five thousand miles apart, and I assure you, they do not get together over Christmas." Again he laughed.

"I see," said Holmes.

"Good, please continue, Mr. Holmes. I have set aside an entire hour of the morning for our meeting, and I am finding it thoroughly entertaining."

"Envoy Munro," Holmes continued, "I am also obliged to state some more serious concern that relates to Mrs. Munro?"

"To Effie? Good heavens. She's a dour Baptist from New Jersey and is currently in Taiwan doing training of the new recruits for the Baptist mission. Who would want to threaten her?"

"No one, sir is threatening her. She herself has become the subject of suspicions."

Mr. Munro gave Holmes a sharp look and then quietly asked, "Is it possible, Mr. Holmes, that your illustrious brother, Sir Mycroft Holmes, was responsible for introducing these suspicions about my wife?"

I had observed Holmes over the years, convincingly lie through his teeth when he considered it useful in the pursuit of criminal conspiracy and wondered what he would now do. He chose to be truthful and forthcoming.

"That is correct, Envoy. Both of us are aware that my brother is something of an *eminence grise* in Whitehall and Westminster."

"Is he now? To those of us in the Foreign Service who have to contend with his interference, he is more commonly known as the 'meddlesome priest.' And that is when we are being charitable."

I could feel the tension in the room rising with that response. The historical reference could not be mistaken, and the image that formed in my mind of the bloated corpse of Mycroft Holmes, all stuck with swords and daggers and lying on the High Altar of Canterbury, was beyond nightmarish.

"He has raised some credible concerns, sir, I assure you."

"Please, then, out with them."

"Are you aware that your wife is carrying on a secretive relationship with a Mr. Lobachevesky, the mathematics teacher at the Friends School?"

"Nicholai Ivanovich Lobachevesky? That imbecile? Good lord, what has that fool been up to now?"

"You know this man?"

"Know him? He was almost a disastrous embarrassment to me. He is a moderately bright math professor from the college in Vladivostok who, instead of teaching his students their algebra, geometry and trig spent every lecture spouting Marx, Kropotkin, Bakunin, and all their silly ilk. He got word that the Czar's boys were about to send him off to a gulag, so he hightails it out of Russia on a fishing scow, lands in Japan, and demands that Great Britain grant him asylum as a poor political refugee. He is nothing more than a raving anarchist. I assume you can appreciate, Mr. Holmes, that His Majesty's government is not having any of that nonsense. And furthermore, we have a good working relationship with the Czar and are not about to be seen to protecting those who are calling for his violent overthrow.

"It was all I could do," he continued, "to get him to be allowed to stay in Japan. I had to beg Sister Biddle and her Quakers to give him a job and then convince the boys at the Diet that he was an enemy of the Czar, and since the Czar happens to be their enemy, nutty Nicky must be their friend. Fortunately, Nick has done not badly at the school. The dear Japanese girls just smile and ignore him if he talks politics; he is not at all bad as a math teacher, and he has found his niche as the coach of their athletic team. I am not surprised that Effie knows him. She is on the board of the school. She knows all the teachers."

"I am not, sir," said Holmes, "concerned with her expected degree of acquaintance with the teachers. I am concerned with an illicit relationship she may be having with Mr. Lobachevesky. And not only that, but they are both involved in a sinister plot to assassinate the Emperor in conjunction with your final yellow ribbon race up Mount Fuji, and I have intercepted documents that substantiate my concern."

Mr. Munro was no longer smiling at Holmes. He was glaring in anger. In a slow, controlled voice, he said, "Holmes, you are impugning the fidelity of my wife. You had better have something to back up your claims, or I will have you thrown out of my Legation and sent packing back to England. Now, either show me what you have or get out."

"Can you account, sir, for the times every fortnight when you're wife is not at home for two or three nights, or for the large sums that appear and are transferred out of her bank account every month?"

The envoy gave Holmes a look of contempt. "No, Mr. Holmes, I cannot and kindly tell me why you think I should be able to? Prior to the day we were married, I had no idea what Effie did or where she was ninety percent of her time and not a clue as to what her income was. Under what sort of antediluvian social arrangement should I expect that to change? I am a married man and her husband, not her owner. May I remind you that, by force of law, as a diplomat, I am forbidden to disclose to her most of what I do or where I go. Why would I expect that she would have any more obligations than I do? Perhaps you, Mr. Holmes, are still of the mind that wives and daughters are mere chattel. I assure you that I am not."

"I have," said Holmes, "an entire file of messages that pertain to your wife and do not reflect well upon her. All of them were sent by your wife to Lobachevesky. One is in code, and we have not been able to decipher it. The rest are in English, replete with affectionate phrases in Russian, and containing discernible references to their plot. Which would you like to see first?"

"Bloody hell, give me the one in code."

"Here it is. The message cannot be understood, but the terms of endearment are obvious, and there is no doubt it was sent by your wife."

He handed the envoy the message that contained so many indecipherable mathematical symbols. Mr. Munro took it and stared at it for half a minute.

"Mr. Holmes, Dr. Watson, would I be correct in assuming that neither of you pursued the study of algebra beyond grammar school? Is that correct? Please, gentlemen, it is a simple question. Your answers, please."

I was not eager to respond but did so first. "I took a class in my first year at medical college, but that was twenty years ago, and I fear I do not remember any of it."

"And I," said Holmes, "have no use for such a study as it does aid in the pursuit of crime."

"Well, gentlemen," the envoy said, "I did study it at Cambridge, and I will tell you that what I am looking at is no more than a standard homework problem in algebra, a quadratic equation that has been solved without resorting to factoring. What you have given me, Mr. Holmes, is some student's homework assignment. I would have expected that Nick would have known how to solve this, but it appears he did not. For the sending of the message, I have no explanation. But the content is meaningless."

He handed the paper back to Holmes, with a sneer on his face.

"Next."

Holmes offered the file with the the remaining correspondence. "All of these messages were sent by your wife to Lobachevesky. You need to read them, and I will be very surprised if you do not find them incriminating."

Mr. Munro took the file and spent the next ten minutes reading through them one by one.

"Would I also be correct," he asked, "in assuming that neither of you speaks a word of Russian beyond *nyet and yah*. Am I correct, gentleman?"

I nodded. Holmes did likewise.

"Well now, it so happens that I do. I had to master it before I sat the Foreign Service exam. So let me instruct you in some basic Russian. The gender of a greeting or compliment is specific to the sex of the person being addressed. The feminine gender is used when addressing a female, and the masculine when addressing a male. Some expressions are neutral. In these notes, there is not a single phrase that is addressed to a male. They are all addressed to a female, except for those that are gender neuter. Whoever Effie sent these messages to, they were not sent to a man. Utterly impossible, Mr. Holmes."

He closed the file and handed it back. I was prepared to walk out of the room in utter shame and embarrassment. Holmes was not yet ready to give in.

"You do not deny, however, Mr. Munro, that the notes are full of terms of endearment, nor that they make reference to your upcoming yellow ribbon event?"

"Are you now suggesting, Mr. Holmes, that my wife might be involved in some unnatural friendship with another woman? I am warning you, sir, men have been shot for less than that."

"What then is your explanation, sir? And how do you explain the references to Fuji, the race, the arrow that breaks the heart of the Emperor?"

Mr. Munro glared back at Holmes. "I do not have one at this moment. What is yours?"

For a few brief seconds, Holmes closed his eyes and touched his fingertips together. Then he jerked his head up and popped his eyes open.

"Of course! They have recruited one of the girls."

"I beg your pardon, Holmes."

"Yes. This now makes perfect sense. These messages were sent to one of the students, one of the seniors who are on the running team. Somehow the teacher and your wife have so twisted the innocent mind of a young woman that she is prepared to win the race, take the arrow from the Emperor, and then use it to murder him. There is no other possible explanation. It is the only one left to us."

"Poppycock, Mr. Holmes. I will wager you ten to one that you are spouting complete nonsense."

Holmes paused for a moment and then replied deliberately. "I accept your wager, sir. For what you have just told me is that you are willing to accept that there is a ten percent chance that I may be right. Are you, sir, sure that you can afford even that degree of risk, given the possible consequences?"

Again the Envoy glared at Holmes for an entire minute without speaking. He then slowly leaned back in his chair and reached for the bell cord and gave it a tug. A moment later a young man, who looked the part of an English secretary, appeared.

"You called, sir?"

"I did, Johnson. Please send an encoded message to Whitehall informing them that I have had a change in my plans and will not be able to attend the meetings in Singapore."

The young fellow looked horrified. "But sir, it's your investiture."

"I know what it is, Johnson. Unfortunately, an emergency has arisen that precludes my attending. Please get that off straight away and it is to remain unknown to anyone else in the legation. Is that understood, Johnson."

"Yes… yes … your Excellency."

The lad looked over at Holmes and me with a hostile expression on his face.

"Very well, Holmes. I will see you on Saturday at the top of Mount Fuji. I will have two Royal Marines with me as snipers, fully prepared to shoot anyone who appears ready to harm the Emperor. That will be all, gentlemen."

He gestured toward the door. We rose in silence and departed.

Chapter Fourteen The Yellow Ribbon

I confess that the blood had departed from my face, and my knees were trembling. Holmes appeared unaffected, except for the quickening of his pace as we marched out of the legation and back to the hotel.

Upon entering our rooms, I immediately grabbed for the brandy bottle and poured myself a stiff one.

"Well, Holmes, this takes the biscuit. God only knows what could happen if the Emperor is assassinated, and it comes out that a Brit and a Russian were in on it."

"Precisely, Watson. Any further insights you might have on this concern would be welcomed."

"Frankly, Holmes, my mind has moved on to matters more pressing."

"And what could those possibly be?"

"Finding Tommy and sorting out how two middle-aged Englishmen get to the top of Mount Fuji without dying several thousand feet below the summit."

Mount Fuji is the highest mountain in Japan and for over a thousand years, has been sacred to the people. It rises, according to the geographers who claim to be able to measure such things, twelve thousand, three hundred and eighty-eight feet above sea level. The mountain's appearance is striking and induces a feeling of awe in those who gaze upon it. The conical shape is nearly symmetrical and is rises far above all of its surroundings. The climb, we were warned, is not for the faint of heart.

Tommy was thrilled when told of our planned hike up the mountain. He spent a full day hustling us all over Tokyo to procure proper footwear, jackets, trousers, hiking sticks, and thick socks. On the Wednesday, he insisted on taking us north the mile or so to the Asakusa neighborhood and the great Senso-ji temple.

"If you expect good fortune on your climb up Fuji-san," Tommy explained, "it is customary to make a prayer and give an offering here before going."

"How interesting," I said. "What am I supposed to do?"

"You buy a stick of incense from the priest, light it, and place it in the sand inside the great kettle. Then you ascend the staircase, face the Buddha, pull on the bell, clap your hands three times, and toss a coin into the box in front of you."

"I suppose I could do that," I said. "But I have no Japanese coins."

"This is not a problem, Doctor-san. The priests accept foreign currency but discount the exchange rate."

I suppose I should have known. I turned to Holmes, smiling, and asked, "Well, Holmes, are you going to contribute a shilling to our good fortune?"

He did not return the smile. "Watson, you know perfectly well that I have no use for superstition either here or in England. This is nothing but stuff and nonsense."

"Holmes," I said, "odds are that you are absolutely right. But a gambler knows to hedge his bets when the stakes are running high." I made my way up the stairs to pay Mr. Buddha.

The following day, Thursday, we boarded the local train and took it as far as the Gotemba station. There we hired a carriage that Tommy had arranged and moved quite quickly along a winding and climbing road. The last mile or two was a series of switchbacks as we ascended the southern slope of the mountain.

"The road takes us to the fifth station," Tommy explained. "This is a great help to climbers. You are already up over six thousand feet before you even have to start. This is good, yes?"

Although I may have forgotten my algebra, I could still do simple arithmetic. If we were at six thousand feet, we only had another six thousand to go. Knowing this did not help my confidence.

We spent the night in a comfortable lodge that, while overpriced, offered decent accommodations and food appropriate to both Japanese and foreigner. We met with the guide and two porters that Tommy had arranged for us and agreed to meet following breakfast the next morning to begin our trek.

"If my understanding is correct," said Holmes the following morning, "we climb today as far as the seventh station, where there is another lodge. We sleep over there and then, very early in the morning, rise and try to make it to the top before sunrise."

"Yes, Sherlock-san" confirmed Tommy. "If we are most fortunate, there will be clear skies, and we will enjoy the sacred experience of watching the sunrise from the top of Fuji-san."

"And what about the Emperor and all the officials and dignitaries?"

"The Emperor," said Tommy, "has already started his ascent. His carriers departed over one hour ago, after he had made a visit to the shrine. A tent is already waiting for him at the summit. He will sleep tonight at the top of Mount Fuji. It is a very special occasion for the nation. He has never done this before. We are most honored to be here and be part of it."

And so our climb began. What astounded me was that the guides and porters began at a snail's pace, plodding one slow, small step after another along the slight incline. I was tempted to shout that we should get a move on but held my tongue. Within an hour, as the pitch of the trail had markedly increased, I thought the pace just fine. After three hours, it occurred to me that I might not mind if we slowed down and took a few more rest stops.

From time to time, as I forced myself to breathe the thinning oxygen as deeply as I could, I took a moment to turn and look out and the vast expanse of land and lakes below me. It was truly stunning, and I looked forward to the experience at the top, assuming that I did not die before getting there.

Holmes, being thin and wiry, was doing somewhat better than I was, but I could see him struggling for breath as well.

"Are you prepared," I asked, "finally to swear off tobacco? It does you no good at a time like this."

Holmes actually smiled at that one. "My dear doctor, it appears you had not noticed that I stopped using it the day we climbed Mount Jinba and have not touched it since. Had I not done so, I might have had to arrange a carrying service like the Emperor, and I do not believe I could have charged the expense and sent the bill to Whitehall."

The open path on which we started had long since disappeared. Now we were climbing up rough-hewn stairs and over volcanic rocks. On many an occasion, I had to reach up with my hands to the rocks above me and climb on all fours. I took to counting my steps and determining that I could do at least two hundred between stops to catch my breath and let my heartbeat subside.

Three, then four, and finally five hours passed since we started. What kept my spirits up was knowing that there was a comfortable lodge up at the seventh station. Assuming that it was of similar quality to the one in which we had passed the previous night, I could look forward to hot tea and some decent food as we sat on the deck and absorbed the unparalleled view in front of us.

"I think I can, I think I can," I kept repeating to myself. And finally, by late afternoon, I could see our lodge, no more than another two hundred feet above me.

As I plodded my weary way up the last few steps, I looked for the deck and chairs on which I could sit and enjoy the spectacular view. There was no deck and no chairs. Some of the climbers who had arrived before me had parked their backsides on the few black rock rocks that were large enough to accommodate them. None of the rocks were flat, and the few that were unoccupied had a shape to them that discouraged anyone from even thinking of sitting down.

The building itself was no more than an elongated shack. Planks were laid down to resemble a floor, hammered willy-nilly in upright positions to form walls, and laid flat and covered with tarpaper to form a roof. I sat down on a bench only to have one of the staff shout rudely at me in Japanese and English, telling me to get off the table. The only place to sit was on the floor. Such an arrangement might be acceptable to a young man or even an older Japanese fellow, but the discomfort that crept into my weary bones after only a few minutes was annoying.

The food that was served was likewise Spartan even by Japanese standards. The portions were small and consisted mostly of cold rice cakes and pickled vegetables. Being famished, I devoured it quickly and then thought I should, like Oliver Twist, ask if there were any more. There was not, and I had to make do with some pieces of fruit that our dear porters had carried all the way up for me.

"Tommy," I whispered, "this is dreadful service. I have not been treated this poorly anywhere in the entire country. How is this tolerated?"

"They have, how do you say, a *monopoly*. This family bought the rights to have the only lodge. They can do what they want and charge whatever they wish. There is nowhere else to stay if you want to be close enough to the top to watch the sunrise."

I had heard of the trust-busting efforts of Theodore Roosevelt and his gang in America as they set out to break up the exploitive monopolies of the oil and railroad companies. Something like that, I thought, would be a good thing on Mount Fuji.

Tommy led us to the 'bedroom' that again caused my spirits to fall. There were no beds, only four large wooden platforms onto which five people each were expected to fit, all packed in like sardines. A mattress, if you can call a one-inch pad a mattress, was provided along with a blanket. Visiting the WC required and treacherous trip outdoors and down a small slope of slippery rock.

I was fairly certain that Holmes was not fairing much better than me. He is, at the best of times, very taciturn and keeps his counsel to himself. He uttered not a word of complaint and appeared to still be absorbed with the monumental case that had been presented to him and about which I had, at least temporarily, ceased to be concerned.

I had slept before in dormitories full of young men who smell and snore, but the last time was over thirty years ago while serving in the Afghan Campaign. A couple of the larger climbers made sounds similar to a Triumph motorcycle starting up six inches from my ear. I was, however, dead tired and involuntarily fell off into a deep sleep.

The next thing I knew, I heard Tommy speaking into my ear and felt his hand rocking my shoulder.

"Doctor John-san. It is time to get up. It is already past three o'clock in the morning. If we want to see the sunrise, we have to leave now."

I truly cannot recall the next twenty minutes, but I came to full consciousness once I stepped outside into the cold night air a few hundred feet below the summit. The wind was light, and the sky was cloudless. I gazed up into the dome of the heavens and was overcome with the beauty of what I was observing. But my moment of reverie was not to last. Torchbearers were interspersed with the climbers, and we began our final ascent like some giant shining centipede crawling up the final stretch of mountain.

Holmes, Tommy, and I found a stretch of flat rock and sat down with our legs folded underneath us and fixed our gaze at the orange glow that was beginning to flow upwards from one spot on the horizon. It became brighter and brighter, and then, suddenly, a brilliant flaming dot of fire appeared. I could hear murmurs all around me as folks from many different nations, languages, and faiths all shared the universal experience of the start of a new day.

"You know, Watson," said Holmes quietly as the circle of the morning sun crept upwards, "At times like this, I could be almost persuaded to be thankful to the divinity that shapes our ends, rough-hew them how we may."

I felt the same way and went so far as to place my hand on the shoulder of my dearest and best friend as we shared the sublime experience.

The moment passed. Soon the sun was fully up, and people were standing and milling about. The hour of five o'clock had already come and gone, and preparations were underway for the arrival of the runners. As I looked around, I could see a warren of small huts, shrines and tents. Some were permanent and had clearly been sitting on the summit for years. Others had most likely been erected the previous day as part of the yellow ribbon event. One rather richly colored tent sat off by itself, and I assumed that it must be where the Emperor Himself was staying.

The runners, I was informed, had already started their race up the mountain at first light. Again the men took off first, followed by the women. As the number of participants allowed to enter had been winnowed down by the first two events and the slower ones all eliminated, the total of men running was only forty, and of women a mere twenty. But those sixty people had to be among the best on the planet at this type of event. The strength, endurance, and determination required were beyond imagining.

Because of the reduced numbers, there would be no heats. The men started in a pack, and thirty minutes later, the women. The race began along the wide, gently sloping trail that I had found so easy early yesterday. By the time they reached the stretch where they would be clambering over the rocks and bounding up the narrow stairs, they would have spread out.

It took a gentleman of my age a full seven hours of climbing to make it from bottom to top. The fastest runners were expected to do it in just under four.

"Tommy," I said, "this is inhuman. No one can keep up a climb like that without stopping for four hours. They will collapse."

"Oh no, Doctor John-san. The officials know this. There are five stations set up along the way. When a runner arrives there, he must stop and wait for five minutes before he is allowed to go again. They are given tea and fruit juice and some rice cakes and sushi if they want it. It is the same for every runner at every station. So it is fair to everyone. But these runners are the best of the best. They will all be fine, Doctor-san."

I hoped he was right.

With three hours to wait, I took out my notebook and began to draft this story that you are now reading. At the time, I still did not know if it would end in an international disaster of the first order, or in the fizzle of an event that never happened.

When there was only an hour left to wait, Holmes, Tommy and I made our way over to one of the larger tents that had been pitched on the rim of the crater. It bore a large Union Jack, and I assumed that it would be packed with officials from what yesterday, at a ceremony in Singapore, was elevated to the rank of our Embassy. Holmes was still the guest of honor and had not had the role of prize-giver snatched away from him in spite of the anger of the invested-*in-absentia* Ambassador. (Reader: I shall henceforth address Mr. Munro by his elevated title.)

The finish line was laid out not far from the Emperor's tent. The winning runners, one man and one woman, would be allowed to cool off and wrapped in a brilliant yellow kimono. They would then be presented to the Emperor, where they would kneel, be awarded the yellow ribbon and medal around their necks, and have the golden arrow placed in their outstretched hands. Then they would walk over to our tent, where Holmes would congratulate them and give them their citation promising a full scholarship to Oxford.

We assumed our places at the front of the British tent. In an inner section, cut off by canvas partitions, I could hear the voice of Grant Munro, but he did not emerge to greet us.

Soon a cry went up. "They're coming! They're coming!"

Our wonderful porters miraculously produced three sets of field glasses from their packs, and we stood at the edge of the mountain looking down. Still, several hundred feet below, the running bodies of a cluster of men could be made out. There was a pack of five of them all running nearly together at the front. Behind them came several other packs and then they spread out. But from the front of the first pack to the last man, there was no more than one hundred yards distance. Anyone of them who had retained enough strength could still win the race.

I watched each of them as they bounced up one set of stairs or pile of rocks after another. I must admit that I was trying to identify the crazy Russian. Somehow I had taken a bit of a liking to Nick, and I was hoping he might defy all odds and win.

I spotted him. He was not difficult to pick out. He was taller than most of the Japanese men, and his pale skin color stood out, but he was well back of the leaders, and I knew that he would have to demonstrate a superhuman effort to move ahead.

Ten minutes later, they had reached the final staircase of unevenly cut steps hewn out of the rock. Three men had pulled away from the rest of the pack and were almost stepping on each other's heels. But there was not enough room for any one of them to pass, the steps being so narrow. One of the fellows was quite tall, the same height or more than Holmes and the same thin body. The other two were shorter, but not one of them had any extra weight on his lithe body.

Now they were almost at the rim of the crater. The final stretch would be a flat sprint along the rim for about one hundred yards to the finish line.

The three leading runners popped up from the final step, all within a fraction of a second of each other and in unison turned and began the sprint to the finish line. The path was wide enough now for them to run abreast, and they looked as if they were joined together, moving like a powerful mass of human flesh. I kept waiting for one of them to pull ahead, but none did. Arms and legs were moving almost in lockstep with each other. The arms were pumping, and the strain on the face was frightening. Then, when they were just three yards from the finish line, and moving at incredible speed, the unthinkable happened. One of them, and no one could say who, tripped. On mass, all three of them fell and tumbled over the finish line, their faces, hands, and shoulders falling into the volcanic cinders. The runners who were immediately behind them jumped to the side or leapt over the fallen bodies, or fell themselves when they tried to avoid the ones who were lying blackened and in pain. Officials scrambled out on to the path and tried to help remove the fallen only to further contribute to the blockade. There was complete mayhem for the next five minutes.

"Good heavens, Tommy. What are they going to do? Who won?"

Tommy seemed oblivious to my near panic. "The officials will have to decide. They will make a decision, and we will all accept it. That is how it is done in Japan."

I watched as several attendants appeared with sponges and buckets and helped the poor fellows clean the grit off their bodies and then assisted each of them in donning a yellow kimono. Another official walked in tentative steps over to the Emperor's tent. After a brief minute in which he appeared to be speaking to someone inside the tent, he returned to the finish line, spoke to the runners, and then led all three of the leaders back to the tent of the Emperor.

"Oh, good," said Tommy. "They will make all of them winners. That is good. Everyone will be happy about that. The Emperor must have ordered it so. He is very wise."

The three fellows came to a spot about ten yards in front of the tent and knelt on the ground. All of them bowed very low and kept their heads and faces down. From out of the tent emerged a man of about my age, wearing a navy blue military jacket, accented with gold epaulets and a red sash. He was accompanied by two chaps that I assumed were his servants. One was bearing a bunch of ribbons with medals attached, and he handed them one after the other to the Emperor. He laid the thick yellow ribbons around the necks of the three men. Then he turned to his other servant and took from him three long gold arrows.

"He came with extras?" I whispered to Tommy.

"Just in case. The Emperor must always be prepared. He cannot be seen to make errors."

The three chaps, with their heads still down, all stretched out their arms with the palms open and facing upwards. Into each pair of hands was laid a golden arrow. As this happened, I could see just how easily any one of them could have grasped onto the shaft and driven the tip into the heart or neck of the Emperor. But it did not happen. They all remained bowed until the Emperor had retreated back into his tent, and then all three of them began to walk, accompanied by older men who I guessed were their proud fathers, directly towards us.

"Oh good heavens, Holmes. You only have one scholarship citation."

A sharp voice spoke from behind me. "We brought extras as well," snarled the British Ambassador. "The Mikado isn't the only one who has to think ahead. Here."

Grant Munro reached over the shoulder of Sherlock Holmes and thrust two more rolled and ribboned documents into his hand, and then he turned and retreated back into the interior of the tent. The three runners, now all beaming through the remaining cinders that had covered them, bowed to Holmes, who bowed back in response and handed each of them one of the rolls. He shook their hands and bowed again. They departed and walked back to the crowd.

They were still on their way when someone shouted, "The women are coming!"

I hustled back to the edge of the mountain and focused the field glasses. Sure enough, in the same stretch as I had first spotted the men, I could see more bodies running. They were more spread out than the men had been. The leader I recognized immediately. It was the same tiny wisp of a woman who had won both the Palace race and the mountain and forest scramble from Takeo to Jinba. If she could keep it up, she would win this one too.

Behind her was a much taller girl. I strained my field glasses on her for several seconds and then lowered them and looked at Holmes. He did the same and looked at me.

"Yes, Watson. She has the name of the Quaker school on her shirt."

"But she has to win before she can do anything."

"She will win. Watch the length of her strides. With no effort, she is keeping up. She is holding back until the end. She has been well trained. She knows exactly what she is doing."

As the two front runners continued to scramble up stairs and along rugged pathways, the distance between them remained the same. Then they reached the final narrow rock staircase where passing was impossible. The small woman pounded her legs like pistons and kept up her pace. There was no way the tall one could pass her.

Or so I thought.

Part way up the stairs, the tall girl jumped out of the staircase and onto the jumbled volcanic rocks. Like a mad mountain goat, she used her long arms and legs, her hands and feet, and scrambled over the rocks, bringing her to the top of the mountain at the same time as the other runner.

Now it was an all-out sprint to the finish line. Watching them run together was like observing a sandpiper running beside a gazelle. The small woman took off like a finely tuned piece of machinery and was soon in front. But the young, tall girl put her head down, pumped her arms, and soon her long legs were moving rapidly, covering more than twice the distance in each stride as her shorter competitor. She passed her, and it was soon obvious that there would be a clear winner and a very worthy and determined runner in second place.

The tall girl crossed the line a full five yards ahead of her rival. She slowed, stopped and fell down on all fours in exhaustion. The girl behind her did the same but then curled up into the fetal position and convulsed with sobs. My heart went out to her, but then my heart stopped.

Approaching the tall girl were a man and a woman, both Europeans. I jerked my field glasses up and then put then down again. I could see Holmes's body stiffen as he stood beside me. On my other side stood Grant Munro. The blood had drained from his face.

Chapter Fifteen   Surprised by Joy

The man and the woman who were attending to the tall runner were the Russian math teacher and the wife of the Ambassador.

Neither Holmes nor I said a thing.

"Marines," said the Ambassador, his voice constricted and faint. "It is possible that any one of those three may attempt to attack the Emperor. If they do, I will give the command, and you will shoot them before they can harm him."

Two Marines knelt and raised their rifles.

"Sir," gasped one of them as he looked through his sites. "Sir, isn't that ..."

"Silence, marine," came the sharp command. "I know who it is, and you will be prepared to shoot if I tell you to."

"Yes, sir. Ready, sir." The lad was trembling.

Mrs. Munro and Nick helped the girl to her feet and into her yellow kimono. Then Nick turned and walked back into the crowd. The girl, with Mrs. Munro by her side, approached the Emperor's tent. The older woman stepped back while the girl knelt, placed her hands on her knees and lowered her head. For nearly thirty seconds, nothing happened. Then the Emperor appeared, again followed by his two servants; one carrying the ribbon and medal and one the golden arrow.

First, the ribbon was placed around her neck. Then, just as the men had done, she held out her hands to receive the arrow. I stopped breathing. I was quite certain that Munro, Holmes, and the Marines did as well. The Emperor released the arrow but did not stand up straight.

"That's good, Mikado, old boy," I heard Mr. Munro whisper to himself. "Now, just back away."

But he did not back away. He placed both his hands on the girl's head, and like a priest with a child at the communion rail lowered his head until it was close to her ear. The tip of the arrow was now no more than a few inches from his heart or his jugular vein. He stayed in that position for some twenty very long seconds and then slowly stood up, turned around, and walked back into his tent.

A collective sound of breaths beginning to be taken could be heard.

"That will be all Marines," said the Ambassador. "Resume your posts. Thank you."

Now Mrs. Munro and the winner of the women's race, a strikingly attractive and exceptionally tall young Japanese girl, were walking directly toward us. When they were only some ten yards off, Mr. Munro suddenly stepped in front of Holmes and snatched the document from his hands.

"I will handle this presentation myself. Thank you, Mr. Holmes. But do not go away. This might interest you."

I was watching the face of Mrs. Munro as the change of men in front of her took place. Her lovely face, in a flash, took on a look of fear, even panic. A second later, she had recovered her composure and walked directly up to her husband.

"Why hello, Jack. This is a surprise. Aren't you supposed to be in Singapore?"

"Fuji has a much better view, darling. And isn't my dear wife supposed to be in Taiwan?"

"The Baptists are just too boring. I'm playing hooky on the last day."

She had only just uttered these words when the beautiful young runner let out a very loud gasp. She then blubbered, speaking with a clear American accent.

"Mom! You ... you ... never told me that my new father was the *ambaaaassador!* Oh, Mom. This is too much. I'm the luckiest girl on earth. I won the race, the Emperor touched me and gave me his blessing, I get to go to Oxford, and my new dad is an ambassador. Oh, wow!"

The girl looked thoroughly lost in amazement but recovered her composure quickly and turned to Mr. Munro and bowed deeply, holding her position as she spoke.

"Most esteemed father, I am honored beyond words to be your daughter. I pledge myself to you and will respect, love and be loyal to you, my father."

She stood up, keeping her head bowed. Then she quickly jerked her head up, and a wide smile spread across her remarkably beautiful face.

"Hello, Daddy. I'm Yuki Victoria. It is an honor to meet you."

She threw her arms around his neck and planted a kiss on his cheek.

Mr. Munro had not uttered a sound. His bewildered gaze wandered back and forth between his wife and the girl.

"Yes, *zaichik moya,*" said Mrs. Munro. "You are truly the child of the moon, and you will go from Fuji on to heaven. But now run along, darling. Your teammates are waiting for you. They won the team prize, and they cannot accept it without you. I will call you when we are ready to start the descent. Now run along."

"Yes, mom."

The girl pulled up her kimono, turned and ran, her long legs flashing with each stride.

"You know, Jack, my darling," said Mrs. Munro. "I really was hoping to save my surprise until we were all back in London. But it seems that the cat is out of the bag, and I am guessing that I have Sherlock Holmes to thank for that. So why don't we all step into your lovely tent? I'm sure you have a pot of tea and some sweets ready, and I am also sure that you would love to have a nice friendly chat."

She strode into the tent and took a seat at one of the small tables. We followed.

"I think," muttered the Ambassador, "that I might need something stronger than tea."

"Johnson," he called, and his secretary appeared. "Would you mind bringing us a bottle of the sake, the *Kōtei no burendo*?"

The young man looked surprised. "Certainly, sir, but isn't that the one you brought in case the Emperor paid us a visit?"

"Well, the old Mikado isn't coming by, and Mr. Holmes here has offered to buy a round. Right, Sherlock? So please bring it over."

The chosen bottle soon appeared. I recognized the brand from having seen it in one of the exclusive shop windows in Ginza. The price was more than my year's income.

"Ah, my dear, wife," said Mr. Munro. "Up to now, you have been a straight-laced Baptist teetotaler. Are you still, or is there another surprise coming?"

"I haven't touched a drop for fifteen years. But perhaps I better have one. Perhaps a generous one."

"Now, my dear, you were about to tell me something." He was not smiling.

"Was I? Oh, yes, about that. Would you like the story from the beginning?"

"That is the recommended place to start most stories, Effie."

"Very well, then. Here it goes." She took a deep breath and a slow swallow of sake. "When I was fifteen years old, the Lord told me that I was to become a nurse and be a medical missionary in Japan. So I went to nursing college, taught myself Japanese, and applied to the Baptist Mission. I was accepted and at age nineteen, found myself in Tokyo. Within a few months, I was speaking Japanese like a native and happily serving the Lord in the mission maternity hospital.

"We were very proud of the hospital. It was all new and shiny and had all the latest American equipment. So we held an open house to show it off to some of the Japanese bigwigs. I chatted with many of them, and they were all impressed by my ability to speak to them in their language and said nice things to me. I thought nothing of it. Men had always said nice things to me, but that was only because I was tall and pretty and American. But the following day, a letter came to the mission office from a General Mutsuhito. He must have been impressed with me because he asked if I could be seconded from the mission to serve on his staff as his English secretary and the governess to his children. I remembered him from the open house. He was the one who was tall and good looking. I don't like peering down on the heads of short men.

"The mission people were all for it. The general was a very important man in the Japanese government. He was the son of some daimyo, and the twenty-third cousin to the last Emperor and in charge of a whole section of the army. I guess that some of my dear Baptists thought I was going to get the general's soul saved, or something. But having me on his staff really did make it less likely that other government officials would give the mission a difficult time.

"The problem was that he lived and worked in Osaka. I did not want to go there all by myself. I knew no one, and I said so. But the men in charge were quite insistent and assured me that my friends could come and visit and if I were really unhappy I could let them know and furthermore, they had prayed about it, and it was the Lord's will that I go there. So I went.

"For the first two months, I was miserable. I was so lonely. The children were bright and lovely and the work helping with English messages and translation was exciting, and I dealt with a lot of secrets of state, but I was ready to send a note back to the mission and tell them that I had to come back to Tokyo, or I was going home to New Jersey. I was that desperate.

"The General, who was as noble a man as ever walked the earth, could see that I was unhappy, and he asked me to have a private dinner with him so we could talk it over. Well, by coincidence, out comes a bottle that is exactly like the one on our table now. Same brand. He poured me a glass, and I tried it, and it was warm and delicious, and I thought it was just Japanese fruit juice, so I had one, then another, and then another.

"The result, as you might have guessed, was that I woke up in the morning in a large bed in an enormous, ornate room, and it was not my bedroom. I wept, knowing that I had become a fallen woman. I did not, for reasons I am not proud of, run away. I prayed the prayer of St. Augustine. You know. 'Lord, make me chaste, but please, Lord, not yet.' So I became the number one mistress to General Mutsuhito. The other women in the household became my friends, and I lived the life of a very privileged young Japanese aristocrat.

"It could not last. I became pregnant and was horrified. I told the General. He was thrilled, and as soon as I began to show he sent a letter to the mission board saying that he had to go to some distant military base and needed me to come with him. We didn't go anywhere, but no one from the mission came to visit me since I was supposed to be way off somewhere in the south islands. When the baby was born, it was a beautiful girl, and at twenty years old, I was a mother. I had all the help I needed and quite enjoyed it. In fact, I loved it.

"That all ended when the war with China broke out. General Mutsuhito led some of the fighting and was killed in action. I was devastated and very frightened. I had no idea what would become of me or my child. But the officers of his family, sort of his attorneys, I guess you would call them, came to me and told me that I was to take my child back to Tokyo and that I would receive a very generous allowance every month to look after the two of us.

"I couldn't arrive on the steps of the mission with my illegitimate child. I couldn't go back home to my family and my home church. They would be ashamed of me. So I went to my closest friend, Esther Biddle, and told her everything. She said not to worry about it, I would not be the first. They had quite a few children at their school who were living with families who were not their parents for all sorts of reasons, and that it could all be arranged easily, especially if I had some money, which I did.

"And I could not lie to my own mother, who was in Jersey all on her own after my dad passed away. So I wrote her a letter and told her everything, and I said she could either disown me or she could enjoy being a grandmother and loving her granddaughter. Well, I had worked in the maternity hospital, and I had seen how mothers and daughters who fought like cats and dogs all of a sudden became friends and loved each other once grandchildren came on the scene. And that was the same with my mom. She came once a year for a long visit and even was here for our wedding. She told me Jack was a good catch, especially for someone my age. Lovely, wasn't she, Jack?"

He had not stopped glaring at her, like an estranged husband in a divorce court, since the story began. Now he stuttered out a response. "You mean to tell me that Thelma, my mother-in-law, knew all about this and didn't let on a word to me? Say it isn't so."

"Of course, it is so, Jack. She's your mother-in-law. She's not going to tell you anything she thinks you don't need to know. Oh, and by the way, she's coming to visit us in London for Christmas.

Well, anyway, Yuki, my daughter, has lived in a home in Minato not far from the school and has grown up there. I visited her for several days every fortnight and taught her both English and Russian, since I speak both, and now she is completely fluent in three languages.

"I really was going to tell you all this, Jack, when we got to London and Yuki was at Oxford, but I couldn't just yet. If my story got out, the dear men at the Baptist mission would have a fit and fire me, and all my work here, that I love, would be lost. What they don't know hasn't hurt them for seventeen years. A few more months won't matter. Your posting here will be up in the fall, and you have to spend a term working at the office in Whitehall before being sent elsewhere, so it was all working out perfectly. Until, of course, along comes Sherlock Holmes and starts asking questions… So, gentlemen, that's my story. Any questions?"

Mr. Munro said nothing and continued to look directly at his wife.

"I do," said Holmes, "have a couple of questions. If you wouldn't mind?"

"Not at all, Mr. Holmes. You are supposed to be a great detective after all, so I guess you like asking questions. And since you started this whole affair you may as well keep going. Oh, but let me have another glass of that sake. Oh my, how I've missed this." She smiled at the bottle and poured herself a second full glass.

"To be fair, madam, this affair began with questions being asked in Whitehall about you."

"Oh, you must mean by your big brother. The one Jack calls the fat twit. Was he behind sending you here?"

"He had a role in it, as did the Second Minister, Mister Humphrey."

"The one Jack calls Dumpty Humpty? What is he saying?"

"He expressed concern over your close connection with a Russian."

"Well he would say that, wouldn't he?"

"Pardon me, madam."

"Humpty is after Jack's job. Everyone in the office knows that. Just watch what he'll try to do now that it's a full Ambassador. And what Russian is he talking about?"

"The mathematics teacher."

She laughed spontaneously. "Nutty Nick? Oh, please, Mr. Holmes. Look, I'm a gal from Jersey. The last thing I want is to get messed up with some crazy Cossak."

Holmes paused, unable to respond to the irrefutable logic. "Very well, Madam, but why did you keep calling your daughter a child of the moon who would break the heart of the Emperor?"

"It was her favorite bedtime story. The fable of the bamboo cutter. You don't know it? It is as famous in Japan as Jack and the Beanstalk is in America or England. You really must read it. It's a lovely tale."

Holmes sighed and reached for his glass of sake.

"I have no more questions. I pass over to you, your Excellency."

Mr. Munro had sat stone-faced since we sat down together.

"Yes, Jack, your turn. I've deceived you and lied to you, and you married a fallen woman. If you want to divorce me, go ahead. I won't try to stop you. But I really do love you, darling."

"Effie," he began in a somber tone, "I am a far from perfect man, but perhaps I am more than you give me credit for. I would like to forgive you and move on with our life, but there is one condition."

Her face fell, and she looked apprehensive. "Yes, Jack. What is that?"

I watched the Ambassador and detected the ends of his lips twitching into a sly smile, and a tiny twinkle flash into his eye.

"You wouldn't happen to have a son hidden away somewhere as well, would you? If I am to be a father, I rather fancy having one of each." His face broke into a wide, loving smile.

She laughed and then smiled sweetly back at him. "No, Jack, I'm sorry, but I do not have one of those to give you…" Here she stopped, lowered her head, and looked up at him with eyes that were more than a little flirtatious. She slowly stroked her top lip with her tongue.

"Or, Jack, I should say, I don't have one … *yet.* But I'm still only thirty-eight. And judging by last weekend, there is nothing wrong with you, darling. So if you want a son, well, you better get busy."

The two of them were now looking goats and monkeys at each other, both of them glowing, and I felt myself beginning to blush.

Mr. Munro rose from his seat and reached his hand across the table to his wife.

"Effie, why not give our daughter a shout, and we'll start back down the mountain."

He then turned to Holmes. "Mr. Holmes, a few days back, I told you that I was a very fortunate man. Having eliminated all other possibilities, I now conclude that I am the luckiest man in the world. Surprised by joy, you could say. Would you agree, Holmes? Oh, and just send your expense claim for the sake to the fat twit in Whitehall."

He was joined outside of the tent by Mrs. Munro, who slipped her arm through his on one side, and his exceptional and beautiful daughter, who did likewise on the other. They began to descend from the mountain.

Holmes sat at the table looking out into the vast expanse of sky, forest, lake, and ocean that we could see on this clear day from the summit of the sacred mountain. He reached his hand into an inside pocket and pulled out his neglected pipe. Slowly he filled it, lit it, and took several slow puffs.

"Watson," said he, "if it should ever strike you that I am seeing only evil where I should see good, that I am getting over-confident in my powers, or that I am blind to what a case deserves, kindly whisper *FUJI* in my ear, and I shall be infinitely obliged to you."

Did you enjoy this story? Are there ways it could have been improved? Please help the author and future readers of New Sherlock Holmes Mysteries by posting a review on the site from which you purchased this book. Thanks, and happy sleuthing and deducing.

About the Author

In May of 2014 the Sherlock Holmes Society of Canada – better known as The Bootmakers (www.torontobootmakers.com) – announced a contest for a new Sherlock Holmes story. Although he had no experience writing fiction, the author, Craig Stephen Copland, submitted a short Sherlock Holmes mystery and was blessed to be declared one of the winners. Thus inspired, he has continued to write new Sherlock Holmes mysteries since and is on a quest to write a new mystery that is inspired by each of the sixty stories in the original Canon. He currently lives and writes in Toronto, Tokyo, and Manhattan. More about him and contact information can be found at www.SherlockHolmesMystery.com.

Dear Sherlockian Readers:

The original Sherlock Holmes story, *The Adventure of the Yellow Face,* involves inter-racial marriage and children of mixed race. It is the closest that The Canon comes to sentimentality. When writing a tribute to it, I borrowed both of those themes.

I wrote this story while living in Japan. It is also a tribute to the country and the many incredible people, both Japanese and ex-pats I was privileged to get to know there.

Here are some of the things I learned more about while doing the reading and research required.

The central historical event in which this story is set, the Russo-Japanese War, took place in 1904 to 1905. The resounding victories of the Japanese on both land and sea led to Japan's becoming recognized as a major world power. Prior to that time, the official offices of both Great Britain and the United States were Legations, headed by Legates or Envoys. Shortly after the end of the war, both countries upgraded their offices to Embassies and the representatives to full Ambassadors.

The references to the events of the war are generally accurate, as are the references to buildings, locations, and related historical events and cultural practices.

References to places visited on route from London to Tokyo are drawn from my privileged past thirty years of world travel and most are tied to events and places I experienced. I had the good fortune to spend time in most of the places mentioned in the story.

The three races described in the story are all along routes I have traveled… walking … during the two years I lived in Japan. Dr. Watson's experience of climbing Mount Fuji is not far removed from mine, except that he got sunshine, and I got a typhoon.

The first Imperial Hotel existed at the time of the events in the story. It was replaced by the stunning creation designed by Frank

Lloyd Wright that opened in 1923 and survived the Great Kanto Earthquake, but was demolished in the 1960s since it occupied too much of the world's most valuable real estate (*So Long ... Frank Lloyd Wright*).

The Suez Canal was built by the French and Egyptians in the 1850s and purchased by Great Britain after the French management company went broke. The British ran it for the next one hundred years.

The Galle Face and the Raffles Hotels are both still in operation, both still fabulously elegant and both places I have been lucky enough to stay at. The Peak Hotel at the top of Victoria Peak is long gone. The Peninsula in Kowloon did not open until well after the dates of this story – pity.

Sherlock Holmes is exceptionally popular in Japan and has many devoted fans and followers. Projecting that popularity back to 1905 was a bit of a stretch.

Gary Punjabi is a real fellow and runs a superb tailoring business, Maclarry Fashions, in Hong Kong. He has been my beloved tailor for thirty years.

Thank you for reading this story. Hope you enjoyed it.

Warm regards,

Craig

More Historical Mysteries
by Craig Stephen Copland
www.SherlockHolmesMystery.com

Copy the links to look inside and download

Studying Scarlet. Starlet O'Halloran, a fabulous mature woman, who reminds the reader of Scarlet O'Hara (but who, for copyright reasons cannot actually be her) has arrived in London looking for her long-lost husband, Brett (who resembles Rhett Butler, but who, for copyright reasons, cannot actually be him). She enlists the help of Sherlock Holmes. This is an unauthorized parody, inspired by Arthur Conan Doyle's *A Study in Scarlet* and Margaret Mitchell's *Gone with the Wind.* http://authl.it/aic

The Sign of the Third. Fifteen hundred years ago the courageous Princess Hemamali smuggled the sacred tooth of the Buddha into Ceylon. Now, for the first time, it is being brought to London to be part of a magnificent exhibit at the British Museum. But what if something were to happen to it? It would be a disaster for the British Empire. Sherlock Holmes, Dr. Watson, and even Mycroft Holmes are called upon to prevent such a crisis. This novella is inspired by the Sherlock Holmes mystery, *The Sign of the Four.* http://authl.it/aie

A Sandal from East Anglia. Archeological excavations at an old abbey unearth an ancient document that has the potential to change the course of the British Empire and all of Christendom. Holmes encounters some evil young men and a strikingly beautiful young Sister, with a curious double life. The mystery is inspired by the original Sherlock Holmes story, *A Scandal in Bohemia.* http://authl.it/aif

The Bald-Headed Trust. Watson insists on taking Sherlock Holmes on a short vacation to the seaside in Plymouth. No sooner has Holmes arrived than he is needed to solve a double murder and prevent a massive fraud diabolically designed by the evil Professor himself. Who knew that a family of devout conservative churchgoers could come to the aid of Sherlock Holmes and bring enormous grief to evil doers? The story is inspired by *The Red-Headed League.* http://authl.it/aih

A Case of Identity Theft. It is the fall of 1888 and Jack the Ripper is terrorizing London. A young married couple is found, minus their heads. Sherlock Holmes, Dr. Watson, the couple's mothers, and Mycroft must join forces to find the murderer before he kills again and makes off with half a million pounds. The novella is a tribute to *A Case of Identity.* It will appeal both to devoted fans of Sherlock Holmes, as well as to those who love the great game of rugby. http://authl.it/aii

The Hudson Valley Mystery. A young man in New York went mad and murdered his father. His mother believes he is innocent and knows he is not crazy. She appeals to Sherlock Holmes and, together with Dr. and Mrs. Watson, he crosses the Atlantic to help this client in need. This new story was inspired by *The Boscombe Valley Mystery.* http://authl.it/aij

The Mystery of the Five Oranges. A desperate father enters 221B Baker Street. His daughter has been kidnapped and spirited off to North America. The evil network who have taken her has spies everywhere. There is only one hope – Sherlock Holmes. Sherlockians will enjoy this new adventure, inspired by *The Five Orange Pips* and *Anne of Green Gables* http://authl.it/aik

. www.SherlockHolmesMystery.com

The Man Who Was Twisted But Hip. France is torn apart by The Dreyfus Affair. Westminster needs Sherlock Holmes so that the evil tide of anti-Semitism that has engulfed France will not spread. Sherlock and Watson go to Paris to solve the mystery and thwart Moriarty. This new mystery is inspired by, *The Man with the Twisted Lip,* as well as by *The Hunchback of Notre Dame.* http://authl.it/ail

The Adventure of the Blue Belt Buckle. A young street urchin discovers a man's belt and buckle under a bush in Hyde Park. A body is found in a hotel room in Mayfair. Scotland Yard seeks the help of Sherlock Holmes in solving the murder. The Queen's Jubilee could be ruined. Sherlock Holmes, Dr. Watson, Scotland Yard, and Her Majesty all team up to prevent a crime of unspeakable dimensions. A new mystery inspired by *The Blue Carbuncle.* http://authl.it/aim

The Adventure of the Spectred Bat. A beautiful young woman, just weeks away from giving birth, arrives at Baker Street in the middle of the night. Her sister was attacked by a bat and died, and now it is attacking her. A vampire? The story is a tribute to *The Adventure of the Speckled Band* and like the original, leaves the mind wondering and the heart racing. http://authl.it/ain

The Adventure of the Engineer's Mom. A brilliant young Cambridge University engineer is carrying out secret research for the Admiralty. It will lead to the building of the world's most powerful battleship, The Dreadnaught. His adventuress mother is kidnapped, and he seeks the help of Sherlock Holmes. This new mystery is a tribute to *The Engineer's Thumb.* http://authl.it/aio

The Adventure of the Notable Bachelorette. A snobbish nobleman enters 221B Baker Street demanding the help in finding his much younger wife – a beautiful and spirited American from the West. Three days later the wife is accused of a vile crime. Now she comes to Sherlock Holmes seeking to prove her innocence. This new mystery was inspired by *The Adventure of the Noble Bachelor.* http://authl.it/aip

The Adventure of the Beryl Anarchists. A deeply distressed banker enters 221B Baker St. His safe has been robbed, and he is certain that his motorcycle-riding sons have betrayed him. Highly incriminating and embarrassing records of the financial and personal affairs of England's nobility are now in the hands of blackmailers. Then a young girl is murdered. A tribute to *The Adventure of the Beryl Coronet.* http://authl.it/aiq

The Adventure of the Coiffured Bitches. A beautiful young woman will soon inherit a lot of money. She disappears. Another young woman finds out far too much and, in desperation seeks help. Sherlock Holmes, Dr. Watson and Miss Violet Hunter must solve the mystery of the coiffured bitches and avoid the massive mastiff that could tear their throats out. A tribute to *The Adventure of the Copper Beeches.* http://authl.it/air

The Silver Horse, Braised. The greatest horse race of the century will take place at Epsom Downs. Millions have been bet. Owners, jockeys, grooms, and gamblers from across England and America arrive. Jockeys and horses are killed. Holmes fails to solve the crime until… This mystery is a tribute to *Silver Blaze* and the great racetrack stories of Damon Runyon. http://authl.it/ais

The Box of Cards. A brother and a sister from a strict religious family disappear. The parents are alarmed, but Scotland Yard says they are just off sowing their wild oats. A horrific, gruesome package arrives in the post, and it becomes clear that a terrible crime is in process. Sherlock Holmes is called in to help. A tribute to *The Cardboard Box.* http://authl.it/ait

The Yellow Farce. Sherlock Holmes is sent to Japan. The war between Russia and Japan is raging. Alliances between countries in these years before World War I are fragile, and any misstep could plunge the world into Armageddon. The wife of the British ambassador is suspected of being a Russian agent. Join Holmes and Watson as they travel around the world to Japan. Inspired by *The Yellow Face.* http://authl.it/akp

The Stock Market Murders. A young man's friend has gone missing. Two more bodies of young men turn up. All are tied to The City and to one of the greatest frauds ever visited upon the citizens of England. The story is based on the true story of James Whitaker Wright and is inspired by, *The Stock Broker's Clerk.* Any resemblance of the villain to a certain American political figure is entirely coincidental. http://authl.it/akq

The Glorious Yacht. On the night of April 12, 1912, off the coast of Newfoundland, one of the greatest disasters of all time took place – the Unsinkable Titanic struck an iceberg and sank with a horrendous loss of life. The news of the disaster leads Holmes and Watson to reminisce about one of their earliest adventures. It began as a sailing race and ended as a tale of murder, kidnapping, piracy, and survival through a tempest. A tribute to *The Gloria Scott*. http://authl.it/akr

A Most Grave Ritual. In 1649, King Charles I escaped and made a desperate run for Continent. Did he leave behind a vast fortune? The patriarch of an ancient Royalist family dies in the courtyard, and the locals believe that the headless ghost of the king did him in. The police accuse his son of murder. Sherlock Holmes is hired to exonerate the lad. A tribute to *The Musgrave Ritual*. http://authl.it/aks

The Spy Gate Liars. Dr. Watson receives an urgent telegram telling him that Sherlock Holmes is in France and near death. He rushes to aid his dear friend, only to find that what began as a doctor's house call has turned into yet another adventure as Sherlock Holmes races to keep an unknown ruthless murderer from dispatching yet another former German army officer. A tribute to *The Reigate Squires*. http://authl.it/akt

The Cuckold Man Colonel James Barclay needs the help of Sherlock Holmes. His exceptionally beautiful, but much younger, wife has disappeared, and foul play is suspected. Has she been kidnapped and held for ransom? Or is she in the clutches of a deviant monster? The story is a tribute not only to the original mystery, *The Crooked Man*, but also to the biblical story of King David and Bathsheba. http://authl.it/akv

The Impatient Dissidents. In March 1881, the Czar of Russia was assassinated by anarchists. That summer, an attempt was made to murder his daughter, Maria, the wife of England's Prince Alfred. A Russian Count is found dead in a hospital in London. Scotland Yard and the Home Office arrive at 221B and enlist the help of Sherlock Holmes to track down the killers and stop them. This new mystery is a tribute to *The Resident Patient.* http://authl.it/akw

The Grecian, Earned. This story picks up where *The Greek Interpreter* left off. The villains of that story were murdered in Budapest, and so Holmes and Watson set off in search of "the Grecian girl" to solve the mystery. What they discover is a massive plot involving the re-birth of the Olympic games in 1896 and a colorful cast of characters at home and on the Continent. http://authl.it/aia

The Three Rhodes Not Taken. Oxford University is famous for its passionate pursuit of learning. The Rhodes Scholarship has been recently established, and some men are prepared to lie, steal, slander, and, maybe murder, in the pursuit of it. Sherlock Holmes is called upon to track down a thief who has stolen vital documents pertaining to the winner of the scholarship, but what will he do when the prime suspect is found dead? A tribute to *The Three Students.* http://authl.it/al8

The Naval Knaves. On September 15, 1894, an anarchist attempted to bomb the Greenwich Observatory. He failed, but the attempt led Sherlock Holmes into an intricate web of spies, foreign naval officers, and a beautiful princess. Once again, suspicion landed on poor Percy Phelps, now working in a senior position in the Admiralty, and once again Holmes has to use both his powers of deduction and raw courage to not only rescue Percy but to prevent an unspeakable disaster. A tribute to *The Naval Treaty.* http://authl.it/aia

A Scandal in Trumplandia. NOT a new mystery but a political satire. The story is a parody of the much-loved original story, *A Scandal in Bohemia*, with the character of the King of Bohemia replaced by you-know-who. If you enjoy both political satire and Sherlock Holmes, you will get a chuckle out of this new story. http://authl.it/aig

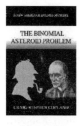

The Binomial Asteroid Problem. The deadly final encounter between Professor Moriarty and Sherlock Holmes took place at Reichenbach Falls. But when was their first encounter? This new story answers that question. What began a stolen Gladstone bag escalates into murder and more. This new story is a tribute to *The Adventure of the Final Problem.* http://authl.it/al1

The Adventure of Charlotte Europa Golderton. *Charles Augustus Milverton* was shot and sent to his just reward. But now another diabolical scheme of blackmail has emerged centered in the telegraph offices of the Royal Mail. It is linked to an archeological expedition whose director disappeared. Someone is prepared to murder to protect their ill-gotten gain and possibly steal a priceless treasure. Holmes is hired by not one but three women who need his help. http://authl.it/al7

The Mystery of 222 Baker Street. The body of a Scotland Yard inspector is found in a locked room in 222 Baker Street. There is no clue as to how he died, but he was murdered. Then another murder occurs in the very same room. Holmes and Watson might have to offer themselves as potential victims if the culprits are to be discovered. The story is a tribute to the original Sherlock Holmes story, *The Adventure of the Empty House.* http://authl.it/al3

The Adventure of the Norwood Rembrandt. A man facing execution appeals to Sherlock Holmes to save him. He claims that he is innocent. Holmes agrees to take on his case. Five years ago, he was convicted of the largest theft of art masterpieces in British history, and of murdering the butler who tried to stop him. Holmes and Watson have to find the real murderer and the missing works of art --- if the client is innocent after all. This new Sherlock Holmes mystery is a tribute to _The Adventure of the Norwood Builder_ in the original Canon. http://authl.it/al4

The Horror of the Bastard's Villa. A Scottish clergyman and his faithful border collie visit 221B and tell a tale of a ghostly Banshee on the Isle of Skye. After the specter appeared, two people died. Holmes sends Watson on ahead to investigate and report. More terrifying horrors occur, and Sherlock Holmes must come and solve the awful mystery before more people are murdered. A tribute to the original story in the Canon, Arthur Conan Doyle's masterpiece, _The Hound of the Baskervilles._ http://authl.it/al2

The Dancer from the Dance. In 1909 the entire world of dance changed when Les Ballets Russes, under opened in Paris. They also made annual visits to the West End in London. Tragically, during their 1913 tour, two of their dancers are found murdered. Sherlock Holmes is brought into to find the murderer and prevent any more killings. The story adheres fairly closely to the history of ballet and is a tribute to the original story in the Canon, _The Adventure of the Dancing Men._ http://authl.it/al5

The Solitary Bicycle Thief. Remember Violet Smith, the beautiful young woman whom Sherlock Holmes and Dr. Watson rescued from a forced marriage, as recorded in *The Adventure of the Solitary Cyclist?* Ten years later she and Cyril reappear in 221B Baker Street with a strange tale of the theft of their bicycles. What on the surface seemed like a trifle turns out to be the door that leads Sherlock Holmes into a web of human trafficking, espionage, blackmail, and murder. A new and powerful cabal of master criminals has formed in London, and they will stop at nothing, not even the murder of an innocent foreign student, to extend the hold on the criminal underworld of London. http://authl.it/al6

The Adventure of the Prioress's Tale. The senior field hockey team from an elite girls' school goes to Dover for a beach holiday … and disappears. Have they been abducted into white slavery? Did they run off to Paris? Are they being held for ransom? Can Sherlock Holmes find them in time? Holmes, Watson, Lestrade, the Prioress of the school, and a new gang of Irregulars must find them before something terrible happens. A tribute to *The Adventure of the Priory School in the Canon.* http://authl.it/apv

The Adventure of Mrs. J.L. Heber. A mad woman is murdering London bachelors by driving a railway spike through their heads. Scotland Yard demands that Sherlock Holmes help them find and stop a crazed murderess who is re-enacting the biblical murders by Jael. Holmes agrees and finds that revenge is being taken for deeds treachery and betrayal that took place ten years ago in the Rocky Mountains of Canada. Holmes, Watson, and Lestrade must move quickly before more men and women lose their lives. The story is a tribute to the original Sherlock Holmes story, *The Adventure of Black Peter.* http://authl.it/arr

The Return of Napoleon. In October 1805, Napoleon's fleet was defeated in the Battle of Trafalgar. Now his ghost has returned to England for the centenary of the battle, intent on wreaking revenge on the descendants of Admiral Horatio Nelson and on all of England. The mother of the great-great-grandchildren of Admiral Nelson contacts Sherlock Holmes and asks him to come to her home, Victory Manor, in Gravesend to protect the Nelson Collection. The invaluable collection of artifacts is to be displayed during the one-hundredth anniversary celebrations of the Battle of Trafalgar. First, Dr. Watson comes to the manor and he meets not only the lovely children but also finds that something apparently supernatural is going on. Holmes assumes that some mad Frenchmen, intent on avenging Napoleon, are conspiring to wreak havoc on England and possibly threatening the children. Watson believes that something terrifying and occult may be at work. Neither is prepared for the true target of the Napoleonists, or of the Emperor's ghost. http://authl.it/at4

The Adventure of the Pinched Palimpsest. At Oxford University, an influential professor has been proselytizing for anarchism. Three naive students fall for his doctrines and decide to engage in direct action by stealing priceless artifacts from the British Museum, returning them to the oppressed people from whom their colonial masters stole them. In the midst of their caper, a museum guard is shot dead and they are charged with the murder. After being persuaded by a vulnerable friend of the students, Sherlock Holmes agrees to take on the case. He soon discovers that no one involved is telling the complete truth. Join Holmes and Watson as they race from London to Oxford, then to Cambridge and finally up to a remote village in Scotland and seek to discover the clues that are tied to an obscure medieval palimpsest. http://authl.it/ax0

The Adventure of the Missing Better Half. Did you ever wonder what happened to Godfrey Staunton, the missing Three-Quarter, after Holmes found him? This story tells you. He met an exceptional young woman, fell in love, and got married. He was chosen to play on England's National Team in the 1899 Home Nations Championship games. Life was good. ... and then it got much worse. Together -- Godfrey Staunton, Dr. Leslie Armstrong, Dr. Watson, and Sherlock Holmes -- must stop an unspeakable crime taking place. This 38th New Sherlock Holmes. A tribute to *The Adventure of the Missing Three Quarter*

The Inequality of Mercy. What happened after Sherlock Holmes and Dr. Watson pardoned Captain Jack Croker for killing Sir Eustace at the Abbey Grange. Have you imagined that he sailed the seven seas for a year and then returned to his beautiful, beloved Mary Fraser? That didn't happen. A year later, murder, treachery, and international intrigue descended on Abbey Grange and, once again, Sherlock Holmes was called upon to bring criminals to justice and assist in the course of true love. Buy the story now, and find out what happened. http://authl.it/bf1

The Adventure of the Second Entente. In June of 1901, a wealthy young nobleman is murdered and yet again Scotland Yard requires help from Sherlock Holmes. The baron has recently returned from an expedition searching for oil in Persia. His only relative and sole heir, a woman from California is the obvious suspect. But then she comes to Sherlock Holmes desperately seeking his help. If she did not kill the man, then who did? Join Holmes, Watson and an unusual woman as they seek to solve the crime and avoid becoming victims themselves. The story is a tribute to the original Sherlock Holmes mystery, *The Adventure of the Second Stain*

Contributions to
The Great Game of
Sherlockian Scholarship

Sherlock and Barack. This is NOT a new Sherlock Holmes Mystery. It is a Sherlockian research monograph. Why did Barack Obama win in November 2012? Why did Mitt Romney lose? Pundits and political scientists have offered countless reasons. This book reveals the truth - The Sherlock Holmes Factor. Had it not been for Sherlock Holmes, Mitt Romney would be president. http://authl.it/aid

From The Beryl Coronet to Vimy Ridge. This is NOT a New Sherlock Holmes Mystery. It is a monograph of Sherlockian research. This new monograph in the Great Game of Sherlockian scholarship argues that there was a Sherlock Holmes factor in the causes of World War I... and that it is secretly revealed in the *roman a clef* story that we know as *The Adventure of the Beryl Coronet.* http://authl.it/ali

Reverend Ezekiel Black—'The Sherlock Holmes of the American West'—Mystery Stories.

A Scarlet Trail of Murder. At ten o'clock on Sunday morning, the twenty-second of October, 1882, in an abandoned house in the West Bottom of Kansas City, a fellow named Jasper Harrison did not wake up. His inability to do was the result of his having had his throat cut. The Reverend Mr. Ezekiel Black, a part-time Methodist minister, and an itinerant US Marshall is called in. This original western mystery was inspired by the great Sherlock Holmes classic, *A Study in Scarlet.* http://authl.it/alg

The Brand of the Flying Four. This case all began one quiet evening in a room in Kansas City. A few weeks later, a gruesome murder, took place in Denver. By the time Rev. Black had solved the mystery, justice, of the frontier variety, not the courtroom, had been meted out. The story is inspired by *The Sign of the Four* by Arthur Conan Doyle, and like that story, it combines murder most foul, and romance most enticing. http://authl.it/alh

www.SherlockHolmesMystery.com

Collection Sets for eBooks and paperback are available at *40% off the price of buying them separately.*

Collection One http://authl.it/al9
The Sign of the Tooth
The Hudson Valley Mystery
A Case of Identity Theft
The Bald-Headed Trust
Studying Scarlet
The Mystery of the Five Oranges

Collection Two http://authl.it/ala
A Sandal from East Anglia
The Man Who Was Twisted But Hip
The Blue Belt Buckle
The Spectred Bat

Collection Three http://authl.it/alb
The Engineer's Mom
The Notable Bachelorette
The Beryl Anarchists
The Coiffured Bitches

Collection Four http://authl.it/alc

The Silver Horse, Braised
The Box of Cards
The Yellow Farce
The Three Rhodes Not Taken

Collection Five http://authl.it/ald

The Stock Market Murders
The Glorious Yacht
The Most Grave Ritual
The Spy Gate Liars

Collection Six http://authl.it/ale

The Cuckold Man
The Impatient Dissidents
The Grecian, Earned
The Naval Knaves

Collection Seven http://authl.it/alf

The Binomial Asteroid Problem
The Mystery of 222 Baker Street
The Adventure of Charlotte Europa Golderton
The Adventure of the Norwood Rembrandt

Collection Eight http://authl.it/at3

The Dancer from the Dance
The Adventure of the Prioress's Tale
The Adventure of Mrs. J. L. Heber
The Solitary Bicycle Thief

Super Collections A and B

30 New Sherlock Holmes Mysteries.

http://authl.it/aiw, http://authl.it/aix

The perfect ebooks for readers who can only borrow one book a month from Amazon

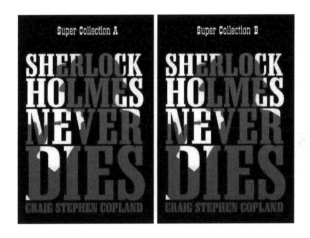

www.SherlockHolmesMystery.com

The Adventure of theYellow Face

The Original Sherlock Holmes Story

Arthur Conan Doyle

The Adventure of the Yellow Face

[In publishing these short sketches based upon the numerous cases in which my companion's singular gifts have made us the listeners to, and eventually the actors in, some strange drama, it is only natural that I should dwell rather upon his successes than upon his failures. And this not so much for the sake of his reputations -- for, indeed, it was when he was at his wits' end that his energy and his versatility were most admirable -- but because where he failed it happened too often that no one else succeeded, and that the tale was left forever without a conclusion. Now and again, however, it chanced that even when he erred, the truth was still discovered. I have noted of some half-dozen cases of the kind the Adventure of the Musgrave Ritual and that which I am about to recount are the two which present the strongest features of interest.]

Sherlock Holmes was a man who seldom took exercise for exercise's sake. Few men were capable of greater muscular effort, and he was undoubtedly one of the finest boxers of his weight that I have ever seen; but he looked upon aimless bodily exertion as a waste of energy, and he seldom bestirred himself save when there was some professional object to be served.

Then he was absolutely untiring and indefatigable. That he should have kept himself in training under such circumstances is remarkable, but his diet was usually of the sparest, and his habits were simple to the verge of austerity. Save for the occasional use of cocaine, he had no vices, and he only turned to the drug as a protest against the monotony of existence when cases were scanty and the papers uninteresting.

One day in early spring he had so fare relaxed as to go for a walk with me in the Park, where the first faint shoots of green were breaking out upon the elms, and the sticky spear-heads of the chestnuts were just beginning to burst into their five-fold leaves. For two hours we rambled about together, in silence for the most part, as befits two men who know each other intimately. It was nearly five before we were back in Baker Street once more.

"Beg pardon, sir," said our page-boy, as he opened the door. "There's been a gentleman here asking for you, sir."

Holmes glanced reproachfully at me. "So much for afternoon walks!" said he. "Has this gentleman gone, then?"

"Yes, sir."

"Didn't you ask him in?"

"Yes, sir; he came in."

"How long did he wait?"

"Half an hour, sir. He was a very restless gentleman, sir, a-walkin' and a-stampin' all the time he was here. I was waitin' outside the door, sir, and I could hear him. At last he out into the passage, and he cries, 'Is that man never goin' to come?' Those were his very words, sir. 'You'll only need to wait a little longer,' says I. 'Then I'll wait in the open air, for I feel half choked,' says he. 'I'll be back before long.' And with that he ups and he outs, and all I could say wouldn't hold him back."

"Well, well, you did you best," said Holmes, as we walked into our room. "It's very annoying, though, Watson. I was badly in need of a case, and this looks, from the man's impatience, as if it were of importance. Hullo! That's not your pipe on the table. He must have left his behind him. A nice old brier with a good long stem of what the tobacconists call amber. I wonder how many real amber mouthpieces there are in London? Some people think that a fly in it is a sign. Well, he must have been disturbed in his mind to leave a pipe behind him which he evidently values highly."

"How do you know that he values it highly?" I asked.

"Well, I should put the original cost of the pipe at seven and sixpence. Now it has, you see, been twice mended, once in the wooden stem and once in the amber. Each of these mends, done, as you observe, with silver bands, must have cost more than the pipe did originally. The man must value the pipe highly when he prefers to patch it up rather than buy a new one with the same money."

"Anything else?" I asked, for Holmes was turning the pipe about in his hand, and staring at it in his peculiar pensive way.

He held it up and tapped on it with his long, thin fore-finger, as a professor might who was lecturing on a bone.

"Pipes are occasionally of extraordinary interest," said he. "Nothing has more individuality, save perhaps watches and bootlaces. The indications here, however, are neither very marked nor very important. The owner is obviously a muscular man, left-handed, with an excellent set of teeth, careless in his habits, and with no need to practise economy."

My friend threw out the information in a very offhand way, but I saw that he cocked his eye at me to see if I had followed his reasoning.

"You think a man must be well-to-do if he smokes a seven-shilling pipe," said I.

"This is Grosvenor mixture at eightpence an ounce," Holmes answered, knocking a little out on his palm. "As he might get an excellent smoke for half the price, he has no need to practise economy."

"And the other points?"

"He has been in the habit of lighting his pipe at lamps and gas-jets. You can see that it is quite charred all down one side. Of course a match could not have done that. Why should a man hold a match to the side of his pipe? But you cannot light it at a lamp without getting the bowl charred. And it is all on the right side of the pipe. From that I gather that he is a left-handed man. You hold your own pipe to the lamp, and see how naturally you, being right-handed, hold the left side to the flame. You might do it once the other way, but not as a constancy. This has always been held so. Then he has bitten through his amber. It takes a muscular, energetic fellow, and one with a good set of teeth, to do that. But if I am not mistaken I hear him upon the stair, so we shall have something more interesting than his pipe to study."

An instant later our door opened, and a tall young man entered the room. He was well but quietly dressed in a dark-gray suit, and carried a brown wide-awake in his hand. I should have put him at about thirty, though he was really some years older.

"I beg your pardon," said he, with some embarrassment; "I suppose I should have knocked. Yes, of course I should have knocked. The fact is that I am a little upset, and you must put it all down to that." He passed his hand over his forehead like a man who is half dazed, and then fell rather than sat down upon a chair.

"I can see that you have not slept for a night or two," said Holmes, in his easy, genial way. "That tries a man's nerves more than work, and more even than pleasure. May I ask how I can help you?"

"I wanted your advice, sir. I don't know what to do and my whole life seems to have gone to pieces."

"You wish to employ me as a consulting detective?"

"Not that only. I want your opinion as a judicious man -- as a man of the world. I want to know what I ought to do next. I hope to God you'll be able to tell me."

He spoke in little, sharp, jerky outbursts, and it seemed to me that to speak at all was very painful to him, and that his will all through was overriding his inclinations.

"It's a very delicate thing," said he. "One does not like to speak of one's domestic affairs to strangers. It seems dreadful to discuss the conduct of one's wife with two men whom I have never seen before. It's horrible to have to do it. But I've got to the end of my tether, and I must have advice."

"My dear Mr. Grant Munro --" began Holmes.

Our visitor sprang from his char. "What!" he cried, "you know my mane?"

"If you wish to preserve your incognito,' said Holmes, smiling, "I would suggest that you cease to write your name upon the lining of your hat, or else that you turn the crown towards the person whom you are addressing. I was about to say that my friend and I have listened to a good many strange secrets in this room, and that we have had the good fortune to bring peace to many troubled souls. I trust that we may do as much for you. Might I beg you, as time may prove to be of importance, to furnish me with the facts of your case without further delay?"

Our visitor again passed his hand over his forehead, as if he found it bitterly hard. From every gesture and expression I could see that he was a reserved, self-contained man, with a dash of pride in his nature, more likely to hide his wounds than to expose them. Then suddenly, with a fierce gesture of his closed hand, like one who throws reserve to the winds, he began.

"The facts are these, Mr. Holmes," said he. "I am a married man, and have been so for three years. During that time my wife and I have loved each other as fondly and lived as happily as any two that ever were joined. We have not had a difference, not one, in thought or word or deed. And now, since last Monday, there has suddenly sprung up a barrier between us, and I find that there is something in her life and in her thought of which I know as little as if she were the woman who brushes by me in the street. We are estranged, and I want to know why.

"Now there is one thing that I want to impress upon you before I go any further, Mr. Holmes. Effie loves me. Don't let there be any mistake about that. She loves me with her whole heart and soul, and never more than now. I know it. I feel it. I don't want to argue about that. A man can tell easily enough when a woman loves him. But there's this secret between us, and we can never be the same until it is cleared."

"Kindly let me have the facts, Mr. Munro," said Holmes, with some impatience.

"I'll tell you what I know about Effie's history. She was a widow when I met her first, though quite young -- only twenty-five. Her name then was Mrs. Hebron. She went out to America when she was young, and lived in the town of Atlanta, where she married this Hebron, who was a lawyer with a good practice. They had one child, but the yellow fever broke out badly in the place, and both husband and child died of it. I have seen his death certificate. This sickened her of America, and she came back to live with a maiden aunt at Pinner, in Middlesex. I may mention that her husband had left her comfortably off, and that she had a capital of about four thousand five hundred pounds, which had been so well invested by him that it returned an average of seven per cent. She had only been six months at Pinner when I met her; we fell in love with each other, and we married a few weeks afterwards.

"I am a hop merchant myself, and as I have an income of seven or eight hundred, we found ourselves comfortably off, and took a nice eighty-pound-a-year villa at Norbury. Our little place was very countrified, considering that it is so close to town. We had an inn and two houses a little above us, and a single cottage at the other side of the field which faces us, and except those there were no houses until you got half way to the station. My business took me into town at certain seasons, but in summer I had less to do, and then in our country home my wife and I were just as happy as could be wished. I tell you that there never was a shadow between us until this accursed affair began.

"There's one thing I ought to tell you before I go further. When we married, my wife made over all her property to me -- rather against my will, for I saw how awkward it would be if my business affairs went wrong. However, she would have it so, and it was done. Well, about six weeks ago she came to me.

"'Jack,' said she, 'when you took my money you said that if ever I wanted any I was to ask you for it.'

"'Certainly,' said I. 'It's all your own.'

"'Well,' said she, 'I want a hundred pounds.'

"I was a bit staggered at this, for I had imagined it was simply a new dress or something of the kind that she was after.

"'What on earth for?' I asked.

"'Oh,' said she, in her playful way, 'you said that you were only my banker, and bankers never ask questions, you know.'

"'If you really mean it, of course you shall have the money,' said I.

"'Oh, yes, I really mean it.'

"'And you won't tell me what you want it for?'

"'Some day, perhaps, but not just at present, Jack.'

"So I had to be content with that, thought it was the first time that there had ever been any secret between us. I gave her a check, and I never thought any more of the matter. It may have nothing to do with what came afterwards, but I thought it only right to mention it.

"Well, I told you just now that there is a cottage not far from our house. There is just a field between us, but to reach it you have to go along the road and then turn down a lane. Just beyond it is a nice little grove of Scotch firs, and I used to be very fond of strolling down there, for trees are always a neighborly kind of things. The cottage had been standing empty this eight months, and it was a pity, for it was a pretty two storied place, with an old-fashioned porch and honeysuckle about it. I have stood many a time and thought what a neat little homestead it would make.

"Well, last Monday evening I was taking a stroll down that way, when I met an empty van coming up the lane, and saw a pile of carpets and things lying about on the grass-plot beside the porch. It was clear that the cottage had at last been let. I walked past it, and wondered what sort of folk they were who had come to live so near us. And as I looked I suddenly became aware that a face was watching me out of one of the upper windows.

"I don't know what there was about that face, Mr. Holmes, but it seemed to send a chill right down my back. I was some little way off, so that I could not make out the features, but there was something unnatural and inhuman about the face. That was the impression that I had, and I moved quickly forwards to get a nearer view of the person who was watching me. But as I did so the face suddenly disappeared, so suddenly that it seemed to have been plucked away into the darkness of the room. I stood for five minutes thinking the business over, and trying to analyze my impressions. I could not tell if the face were that of a man or a woman. It had been too far from me for that. But its color was what had impressed me most. It was of a livid chalky white, and with something set and rigid about it which was shockingly unnatural. So disturbed was I that I determined to see a little more of the new inmates of the cottage. I approached and knocked at the door, which was instantly opened by a tall, gaunt woman with a harsh, forbidding face.

"'What may you be wantin'?' she asked, in a Northern accent.

"'I am your neighbor over yonder,' said I, nodding towards my house. 'I see that you have only just moved in, so I thought that if I could be of any help to you in any -- '

"'Ay, we'll just ask ye when we want ye,' said she, and shut the door in my face. Annoyed at the churlish rebuff, I turned my back and walked home. All evening, though I tried to think of other things, my mind would still turn to the apparition at the window and the rudeness of the woman. I determined to say nothing about the former to my wife, for she is a nervous, highly strung woman, and I had no wish that she would share the unpleasant impression which had been produced upon myself. I remarked to her, however, before I fell asleep, that the cottage was now occupied, to which she returned no reply.

"I am usually an extremely sound sleeper. It has been a standing jest in the family that nothing could ever wake me during the night. And yet somehow on that particular night, whether it may have been the slight excitement produced by my little adventure or not I know not, but I slept much more lightly than usual. Half in my dreams I was dimly conscious that something was going on in the room, and gradually became aware that my wife had dressed herself and was slipping on her mantle and her bonnet. My lips were parted to murmur out some sleepy words of surprise or remonstrance at this untimely preparation, when suddenly my half-opened eyes fell upon her face, illuminated by the candle-light, and astonishment held me dumb. She wore an expression such as I had never seen before -

- such as I should have thought her incapable of assuming. She was deadly pale and breathing fast, glancing furtively towards the bed as she fastened her mantle, to see if she had disturbed me. Then, thinking that I was still asleep, she slipped noiselessly from the room, and an instant later I heard a sharp creaking which could only come from the hinges of the front door. I sat up in bed and rapped my knuckles against the rail to make certain that I was truly awake. Then I took my watch from under the pillow. It was three in the morning. What on this earth could my wife be doing out on the country road at three in the morning?

"I had sat for about twenty minutes turning the thing over in my mind and trying to find some possible explanation. The more I thought, the ore extraordinary and inexplicable did it appear. I was still puzzling over it when I heard the door gently close again, and her footsteps coming up the stairs.

"'Where in the world have you been, Effie?' I asked as she entered.

"She gave a violent start and a kind of gasping cry when I spoke, and that cry and start troubled me more than all the rest, for there was something indescribably guilty about them. My wife had always been a woman of a frank, open nature, and it gave me a chill to see her slinking into her own room, and crying out and wincing when her own husband spoke to her.

"'You awake, Jack!' she cried, with a nervous laugh. 'Why, I thought that nothing could awake you.'

"'Where have you been?' I asked, more sternly.

178

"'I don't wonder that you are surprised,' said she, and I could see that her fingers were trembling as she undid the fastenings of her mantle. 'Why, I never remember having done such a thing in my life before. The fact is that I felt as though I were choking, and had a perfect longing for a breath of fresh air. I really think that I should have fainted if I had not gone out. I stood at the door for a few minutes, and now I am quite myself again.'

"All the time that she was telling me this story she never once looked in my direction, and her voice was quite unlike her usual tones. It was evident to me that she was saying what was false. I said nothing in reply, but turned my face to the wall, sick at heart, with my mind filled with a thousand venomous doubts and suspicions. What was it that my wife was concealing from me? Where had she been during that strange expedition? I felt that I should have no peace until I knew, and yet I shrank from asking her again after once she had told me what was false. All the rest of the night I tossed and tumbled, framing theory after theory, each more unlikely than the last.

"I should have gone to the City that day, but I was too disturbed in my mind to be able to pay attention to business matters. My wife seemed to be as upset as myself, and I could see from the little questioning glances which she kept shooting at me that she understood that I disbelieved her statement, and that she was at her wits' end what to do. We hardly exchanged a word during breakfast, and immediately afterwards I went out for a walk, that I might think the matter out in the fresh morning air.

"I went as far as the Crystal Palace, spent an hour in the grounds, and was back in Norbury by one o'clock. It happened that my way took me past the cottage, and I stopped for an instant to look at the windows, and to see if I could catch a glimpse of the strange face which had looked out at me on the day before. As I stood there, imagine my surprise, Mr. Holmes, when the door suddenly opened and my wife walked out.

"I was struck dumb with astonishment at the sight of her; but my emotions were nothing to those which showed themselves upon her face when our eyes met. She seemed for an instant to wish to shrink back inside the house again; and then, seeing how useless all concealment must be, she came forward, with a very white face and frightened eyes which belied the smile upon her lips.

"'Ah, Jack,' she said, 'I have just been in to see if I can be of any assistance to our new neighbors. Why do you look at me like that, Jack? You are not angry with me?'

"'So,' said I, 'this is where you went during the night.'

"'What do you mean?" she cried.

"'You came here. I am sure of it. Who are these people, that you should visit them at such an hour?'

"'I have not been here before.'

"'How can you tell me what you know is false?' I cried. 'Your very voice changes as you speak. When have I ever had a secret from you? I shall enter that cottage, and I shall probe the matter to the bottom.'

"'No, no, Jack, for God's sake!' she gasped, in uncontrollable emotion. Then, as I approached the door, she seized my sleeve and pulled me back with convulsive strength.

"'I implore you not to do this, Jack,' she cried. 'I swear that I will tell you everything some day, but nothing but misery can come of it if you enter that cottage.' Then, as I tried to shake her off, she clung to me in a frenzy of entreaty.

"'Trust me, Jack!' she cried. 'Trust me only this once. You will never have cause to regret it. You know that I would not have a secret from you if it were not for your own sake. Our whole lives are at stake in this. If you come home with me, all will be well. If you force your way into that cottage, all is over between us.'

"There was such earnestness, such despair, in her manner that her words arrested me, and I stood irresolute before the door.

"'I will trust you on one condition, and on one condition only,' said I at last. 'It is that this mystery comes to an end from now. You are at liberty to preserve your secret, but you must promise me that there shall be no more nightly visits, no more doings which are kept from my knowledge. I am willing to forget those which are passed if you will promise that there shall be no more in the future.'

"'I was sure that you would trust me,' she cried, with a great sigh of relief. 'It shall be just as you wish. Come away -- oh, come away up to the house.'

"Still pulling at my sleeve, she led me away from the cottage. As we went I glanced back, and there was that yellow livid face watching us out of the upper window. What link could there be between that creature and my wife? Or how could the coarse, rough woman whom I had seen the day before be connected with her? It was a strange puzzle, and yet I knew that my mind could never know ease again until I had solved it.

"For two days after this I stayed at home, and my wife appeared to abide loyally by our engagement, for, as far as I know, she never stirred out of the house. On the third day, however, I had ample evidence that her solemn promise was not enough to hold her back from this secret influence which drew her away from her husband and her duty.

"I had gone into town on that day, but I returned by the 2.40 instead of the 3.36, which is my usual train. As I entered the house the maid ran into the hall with a startled face.

"'Where is your mistress?' I asked.

"'I think that she has gone out for a walk,' she answered.

"My mind was instantly filled with suspicion. I rushed upstairs to make sure that she was not in the house. As I did so I happened to glance out of one of the upper windows, and saw the maid with whom I had just been speaking running across the field in the direction of the cottage. Then of course I saw exactly what it all meant. My wife had gone over there, and had asked the servant to call her if I should return. Tingling with anger, I rushed down and hurried across, determined to end the matter once and forever. I saw my wife and the maid hurrying back along the lane, but I did not stop to speak with them. In the cottage lay the secret which was casting a shadow over my life. I vowed that, come what might, it should be a secret no longer. I did not even knock when I reached it, but turned the handle and rushed into the passage.

"It was all still and quiet upon the ground floor. In the kitchen a kettle was singing on the fire, and a large black cat lay coiled up in the basket; but there was no sign of the woman whom I had seen before. I ran into the other room, but it was equally deserted. Then I rushed up the stairs, only to find two other rooms empty and deserted at the top. There was no one at all in the whole house. The furniture and pictures were of the most common and vulgar description, save in the one chamber at the window of which I had seen the strange face. That was comfortable and elegant, and all my suspicions rose into a fierce bitter flame when I saw that on the mantelpiece stood a copy of a fell-length photograph of my wife, which had been taken at my request only three months ago.

"I stayed long enough to make certain that the house was absolutely empty. Then I left it, feeling a weight at my heart such as I had never had before. My wife came out into the hall as I entered my house; but I was too hurt and angry to speak with her, and pushing past her, I made my way into my study. She followed me, however, before I could close the door.

"'I am sorry that I broke my promise, Jack,' said she; 'but if you knew all the circumstances I am sure that you would forgive me.'

"'Tell me everything, then,' said I.

"'I cannot, Jack, I cannot,' she cried.

"'Until you tell me who it is that has been living in that cottage, and who it is to whom you have given that photograph, there can never be any confidence between us,' said I, and breaking away from her, I left the house. That was yesterday, Mr. Holmes, and I have not seen her since, nor do I know anything more about this strange business. It is the first shadow that has come between us, and it has so shaken me that I do not know what I should do for the best. Suddenly this morning it occurred to me that you were the man to advise me, so I have hurried to you now, and I place myself unreservedly in your hands. If there is any point which I have not made clear, pray question me about it. But, above all, tell me quickly what I am to do, for this misery is more than I can bear."

Holmes and I had listened with the utmost interest to this extraordinary statement, which had been delivered in the jerky, broken fashion of a man who is under the influence of extreme emotions. My companion sat silent for some time, with his chin upon his hand, lost in thought.

"Tell me," said he at last, "could you swear that this was a man's face which you saw at the window?"

"Each time that I saw it I was some distance away from it, so that it is impossible for me to say."

"You appear, however, to have been disagreeably impressed by it."

"It seemed to be of an unnatural color, and to have a strange rigidity about the features. When I approached, it vanished with a jerk."

"How long is it since your wife asked you for a hundred pounds?"

"Nearly two months."

"Have you ever seen a photograph of her first husband?"

"No; there was a great fire at Atlanta very shortly after his death, and all her papers were destroyed."

"And yet she had a certificate of death. You say that you saw it."

"Yes; she got a duplicate after the fire."

"Did you ever meet any one who knew her in America?"

"No."

"Did she ever talk of revisiting the place?"

"No."

"Or get letters from it?"

"No."

"Thank you. I should like to think over the matter a little now. If the cottage is now permanently deserted we may have some difficulty. If, on the other hand, as I fancy is more likely, the inmates were warned of you coming, and left before you entered yesterday, then they may be back now, and we should clear it all up easily. Let me advise you, then, to return to Norbury, and to examine the windows of the cottage again. If you have reason to believe that is inhabited, do not force your way in, but send a wire to my friend and me. We shall be with you within an hour of receiving it, and we shall then very soon get to the bottom of the business."

"And if it is still empty?"

"In that case I shall come out to-morrow and talk it over with you. Good-by; and, above all, do not fret until you know that you really have a cause for it."

"I am afraid that this is a bad business, Watson," said my companion, as he returned after accompanying Mr. Grant Munro to the door. "What do you make of it?"

"It had an ugly sound," I answered.

"Yes. There's blackmail in it, or I am much mistaken."

"And who is the blackmailer?"

"Well, it must be the creature who lives in the only comfortable room in the place, and has her photograph above his fireplace. Upon my word, Watson, there is something very attractive about that livid face at the window, and I would not have missed the case for worlds."

"You have a theory?"

"Yes, a provisional one. But I shall be surprised if it does not turn out to be correct. This woman's first husband is in that cottage."

"Why do you think so?"

"How else can we explain her frenzied anxiety that her second one should not enter it? The facts, as I read them, are something like this: This woman was married in America. Her husband developed some hateful qualities; or shall we say that he contracted some loathsome disease, and became a leper or an imbecile? She flies from him at last, returns to England, changes her name, and starts her life, as she thinks, afresh. She has been married three years, and believes that her position is quite secure, having shown her husband the death certificate of some man whose name she has assumed, when suddenly her whereabouts is discovered by her first husband; or, we may suppose, by some unscrupulous woman who has attached herself to the invalid. They write to the wife, and threaten to come and expose her. She asks for a hundred pounds, and endeavors to buy them off. They come in spite of it, and when the husband mentions casually to the wife that there a new-comers in the cottage, she knows in some way that they are her pursuers. She waits until her husband is asleep, and then she rushes down to endeavor to persuade them to leave her in peace. Having no success, she goes again next morning, and her husband meets her, as he has told us, as she comes out. She promises him then not to go there again, but two days afterwards the hope of getting rid of those dreadful neighbors was too strong for her, and she made another attempt, taking down with her the photograph which had probably been demanded from her. In the midst of this interview the maid rushed in to say that the master had come home, on which the wife, knowing that he would come straight down to the cottage, hurried the inmates out at the back door, into the grove of fir-trees, probably, which was mentioned as standing near. In this way he found the place deserted. I shall be very much surprised, however, if it still so when he reconnoitres it this evening. What do you think of my theory?"

"It is all surmise."

"But at least it covers all the facts. When new facts come to our knowledge which cannot be covered by it, it will be time enough to reconsider it. We can do nothing more until we have a message from our friend at Norbury."

But we had not a very long time to wait for that. It came just as we had finished our tea. "The cottage is still tenanted," it said. "Have seen the face again at the window. Will meet the seven o'clock train, and will take no steps until you arrive."

He was waiting on the platform when we stepped out, and we could see in the light of the station lamps that he was very pale, and quivering with agitation.

"They are still there, Mr. Holmes," said he, laying his hand hard upon my friend's sleeve. "I saw lights in the cottage as I came down. We shall settle it now once and for all."

"What is your plan, then?" asked Holmes, as he walked down the dark tree-lined road.

"I am going to force my way in and see for myself who is in the house. I wish you both to be there as witnesses."

"You are quite determined to do this, in spite of your wife's warning that it is better that you should not solve the mystery?"

"Yes, I am determined."

"Well, I think that you are in the right. Any truth is better than indefinite doubt. We had better go up at once. Of course, legally, we are putting ourselves hopelessly in the wrong; but I think that it is worth it."

It was a very dark night, and a thin rain began to fall as we turned from the high road into a narrow lane, deeply rutted, with hedges on either side. Mr. Grant Munro pushed impatiently forward, however, and we stumbled after him as best we could.

"There are the lights of my house," he murmured, pointing to a glimmer among the trees. "And here is the cottage which I am going to enter."

We turned a corner in the lane as he spoke, and there was the building close beside us. A yellow bar falling across the black foreground showed that the door was not quite closed, and one window in the upper story was brightly illuminated. As we looked, we saw a dark blur moving across the blind.

"There is that creature!" cried Grant Munro. "You can see for yourselves that some one is there. Now follow me, and we shall soon know all."

We approached the door; but suddenly a woman appeared out of the shadow and stood in the golden track of the lamp-light. I could not see her face in the he darkness, but her arms were thrown out in an attitude of entreaty.

"For God's sake, don't Jack!" she cried. "I had a presentiment that you would come this evening. Think better of it, dear! Trust me again, and you will never have cause to regret it."

"I have trusted you tool long, Effie," he cried, sternly. "Leave go of me! I must pass you. My friends and I are going to settle this matter once and forever!" He pushed her to one side, and we followed closely after him. As he threw the door open an old woman ran out in front of him and tried to bar his passage, but he thrust her back, and an instant afterwards we were all upon the stairs. Grant Munro rushed into the lighted room at the top, and we entered at his heels.

It was a cosey, well-furnished apartment, with two candles burning upon the table and two upon the mantelpiece. In the corner, stooping over a desk, there sat what appeared to be a little girl. Her face was turned away as we entered, but we could see that she was dressed in a red frock, and that she had long white gloves on. As she whisked round to us, I gave a cry of surprise and horror. The face which she turned towards us was of the strangest livid tint, and the features were absolutely devoid of any expression. An instant later the mystery was explained. Holmes, with a laugh, passed his hand behind the child's ear, a mask peeled off from her countenance, an there was a little coal black negress, with all her white teeth flashing in amusement at our amazed faces. I burst out laughing, out of sympathy with her merriment; but Grant Munro stood staring, with his hand clutching his throat.

"My God!" he cried. "What can be the meaning of this?"

"I will tell you the meaning of it," cried the lady, sweeping into the room with a proud, set face. "You have forced me, against my own judgment, to tell you, and now we must both make the best of it. My husband died at Atlanta. My child survived."

"Your child?"

She drew a large silver locket from her bosom. "You have never seen this open."

"I understood that it did not open."

She touched a spring, and the front hinged back. There was a portrait within of a man strikingly handsome and intelligent-looking, but bearing unmistakable signs upon his features of his African descent.

"That is John Hebron, of Atlanta," said the lady, "and a nobler man never walked the earth. I cut myself off from my race in order to wed him, but never once while he lived did I for an instant regret it. It was our misfortune that our only child took after his people rather than mine. It is often so in such matches, and little Lucy is darker far than ever her father was. But dark or fair, she is my own dear little girlie, and her mother's pet." The little creature ran across at the words and nestled up against the lady's dress. "When I left her in America,"

191

she continued, "it was only because her health was weak, and the change might have done her harm. She was given to the care of a faithful Scotch woman who had once been our servant. Never for an instant did I dream of disowning her as my child. But when chance threw you in my way, Jack, and I learned to love you, I feared to tell you about my child. God forgive me, I feared that I should lose you, and I had not the courage to tell you. I had to choose between you, and in my weakness I turned away from my own little girl. For three years I have kept her existence a secret from you, but I heard from the nurse, and I knew that all was well with her. At last, however, there came an overwhelming desire to see the child once more. I struggled against it, but in vain. Though I knew the danger, I determined to have the child over, if it were but for a few weeks. I sent a hundred pounds to the nurse, and I gave her instructions about this cottage, so that she might come as a neighbor, without my appearing to be in any way connected with her. I pushed my precautions so far as to order her to keep the child in the house during the daytime, and to cover up her little face and hands so that even those who might see her at the window should not gossip about there being a black child in the neighborhood. If I had been less cautious I might have been more wise, but I was half crazy with fear that you should learn the truth.

"It was you who told me first that the cottage was occupied. I should have waited for the morning, but I could not sleep for excitement, and so at last I slipped out, knowing how difficult it is to awake you. But you saw me go, and that was the beginning of my troubles. Next day you had my secret at your mercy, but you nobly refrained from pursuing your advantage. Three days later, however, the nurse and child only just escaped from the back door as you rushed in at the front one. And now to-night you at last know all, and I ask you what is to become of us, my child and me?" She clasped her hands and waited for an answer.

It was a long ten minutes before Grant Munro broke the silence, and when his answer came it was one of which I love to think. He lifted the little child, kissed her, and then, still carrying her, he held his other hand out to his wife and turned towards the door.

"We can talk it over more comfortably at home," said he. "I am not a very good man, Effie, but I think that I am a better one than you have given me credit for being."

Holmes and I followed them down the lane, and my friend plucked at my sleeve as we came out.

"I think," said he, "that we shall be of more use in London than in Norbury."

Not another word did he say of the case until late that night, when he was turning away, with his lighted candle, for his bedroom.

"Watson," said he, "if it should ever strike you that I am getting a little over-confident in my powers, or giving less pains to a case than it deserves, kindly whisper 'Norbury' in my ear, and I shall be infinitely obliged to you."

Printed in Great Britain
by Amazon